THE STORY SO FAR

After the death of the man she believed was her father, Gemma Smith had left the opal fields of the outback for Sydney to find out the truth about her mother, and to sell her priceless discovery, a flawless black opal. Fate had introduced her to Nathan Whitmore, a famous playwright, who offered her a reward for the gem, which had been stolen from his adoptive father twenty years before. Nathan seduced and married Gemma, and her life changed forever; she witnessed startling changes in the Whitmore household, too: Nathan's wild-child adoptive sister, Jade, discovered happiness with Kyle Gainsford, while Melanie, the family housekeeper, had been swept off in the arms of Royce Grantham. And just look what had happened between Ava, Byron's much younger sister, and Vince Morelli! But, best of all, Gemma had found her real mother and father right on her own doorstep: it was hard to believe that she was the result of a never-dying love between Celeste Campbell and Byron Whitmore!

However, Gemma's marriage to Nathan was falling apart. It seemed that the gossips were right, and that her husband didn't have a heart. But miracles had already happened for Gemma and those around her; was it too much to ask for just one more?

D0048469

Dear Reader,

Welcome to the sixth book in a totally compelling family saga, set in the glamorous, cutthroat world of opal dealing in Australia.

Laden with dark secrets, forbidden desires, scandalous discoveries and happy endings, HEARTS OF FIRE has unfolded over a series of six books. Beautiful, innocent Gemma Smith goes in search of a new life, and fate introduces her to Nathan Whitmore, the ruthless, talented and utterly controlled screenwriter and heir to the Whitmore opal fortune.

Throughout the series, Gemma has discovered the truth about Nathan, seduction, her real mother and the priceless Black Opal. But, at the same time, each novel is an independent, fully developed romance that can be read on its own, revealing the passion, deception and hope that has existed between two fabulously rich clans over twenty tempestuous years.

HEARTS OF FIRE has been especially written by one of romance fiction's rising stars for you to enjoy—we're sure you will!

THE EDITOR

MIRANDA LEE

Marriage & Miracles

Harlequin Books

TORONTO • NEW YORK • LONDON
AMSTERDAM • PARIS • SYDNEY • HAMBURG
STOCKHOLM • ATHENS • TOKYO • MILAN
MADRID • WARSAW • BUDAPEST • AUCKLAND

ISBN 0-373-11784-1

MARRIAGE & MIRACLES

First North American Publication 1995.

PRINCIPAL CHARACTERS IN THIS BOOK

GEMMA WHITMORE-SMITH: when the man who she believed was her father died, Gemma discovered a priceless black opal, the Heart of Fire, and a photograph that cast doubt on her real identity. In search of her mother and a new life, she went to Sydney, where she was seduced by, and then married to, Nathan Whitmore. Happily, Gemma eventually unearthed the secret of the Heart of Fire, and who her real parents were: Celeste Campbell and Byron Whitmore, Nathan's adoptive father! But now her marriage to Nathan is in tatters, because it seems he is unable to return her love....

NATHAN WHITMORE: adopted son of Byron Whitmore, Nathan is a talented, successful playwright. But, after a desperately troubled childhood and a divorce, Nathan is utterly ruthless and emotionally controlled. Can he rediscover his heart and save his marriage?

CELESTE CAMPBELL: head of the Campbell Jewels empire, Celeste was seen as a bright, beautiful predator who was not to be toyed with, in business or in love. But her brittle exterior hid a turbulent past and a broken heart—until she found love again with Byron Whitmore, who had always been the only man for her, and Gemma, her long-lost daughter.

BYRON WHITMORE: patriarch and head of the Whitmore family. His first unhappy marriage to Irene came to a thankful, though tragic end. Then fate reintroduced him to Celeste, the only woman he ever came close to loving, and he discovered that he had another daughter—Gemma.

DAMIAN CAMPBELL: younger brother of Celeste, Damian is interested only in self-gratification and sexual pleasure.... He doesn't care whom he hurts in their pursuit....

LENORE LANGTRY: talented stage actress, ex-wife of Nathan Whitmore and mother of Kirsty, Lenore has finally found love with top lawyer, Zachary Marsden.

A NOTE TO THE READER:
This novel is one of six set in the glamorous, cutthroat world of Australian opal dealing. Each novel is independent and can be read on its own. It is the author's suggestion, however, that they be read in the order written.

FAMILY TREE

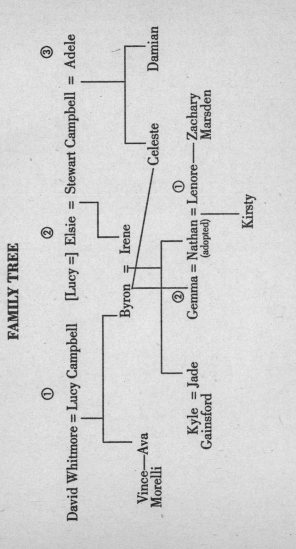

① ② ③

David Whitmore = Lucy Campbell   [Lucy =] Elsie = Stewart Campbell = Adele

Vince—Ava
Morelli

Byron = Irene

Irene

Celeste   Damian

Kyle = Jade
Gainsford

② Gemma = Nathan = Lenore——Zachary
(adopted)   Marsden

①

Kirsty

CHAPTER ONE

THE première of a new play by Nathan Whitmore had become quite an event in Sydney over the past few years. It was nothing to see the Prime Minister of Australia as well as other heads of state roll up with their wives, not to mention a good supply of the sort of socialites and celebrities who graced the pages of the tabloids and women's magazines every other week.

Gemma surveyed the famous faces in the crowd gathered in the foyer with a sincere lack of interest or awe. Fame as such did not impress her. Why should it? There was a time—not very long ago—when she would not have recognised a single famous face here tonight, and her life had not been any the less for it.

'Smile, Mrs Whitmore,' one of the plethora of photographers directed her way. 'And you too, Ms Campbell.'

'Smile, Gemma,' Celeste hissed under her breath. 'This was your idea, remember? I did warn you not to come, but now that you're here, you must grin and bear it.'

Both women smiled and Gemma wondered what the photographer would say if he knew he was not just taking a photograph of Ms Celeste Campbell and Mrs Nathan Whitmore, but mother and daughter.

There was no doubt that the news would set Sydney's social set on its ear, especially if it were also publicly revealed that Gemma's father-in-law, Byron Whitmore, was Gemma's biological father as well.

The long-standing feud between the glamorous lady boss of Campbell Jewels and the handsome head of Whitmore Opals had fuelled many a discussion over the years. An affair gone sour had been whispered at occasionally, but no

one could have guessed at the extraordinary set of circumstances which had brought about Gemma's birth, her sub-
sequent stealing as a baby by a man who thought he was her
father, but who wasn't, and her final return into the lives of
her real parents twenty years later.

It had only been three days since Gemma had found out
the truth, yet already she had forged a bond with her father
and mother that was astonishingly close and full of love.
They were both tremendous people, in her opinion. Not
saints, of course, either of them, but basically good souls
with deeply caring natures who only wanted the best for
their long-lost daughter. The added news that they were finally going to get married had made Gemma very happy.

Her own marriage was another matter . . .

Gemma's stomach began churning. Her plan to get Nathan back had seemed a good one in theory. In practice, it
was dangerous and risky and nerve-racking. But what alternative did she have? She loved Nathan more than life itself and felt sure that he loved her back, despite everything.
She couldn't let cruel twists of fate and unfortunate mis-
understandings destroy their marriage. Certainly not now,
when she might possibly be pregnant.

'What's taking Byron so long?' she said worriedly after
the photographer had scuttled away. 'I hope he's not trying
to play peace-maker between Nathan and me. I asked him
not to meddle.'

'Please give Byron more credit for intelligence than that,
Gemma. He realises any influence he has over Nathan is at
a low ebb at the moment. Nathan was far from impressed
to find out Byron had slept with me while he was still a
married man. Then when he added that we were going to get
married . . .' Celeste's eyes rolled expressively. 'He said Nathan stared at him as though he were mad.'

Gemma sighed. 'Poor Byron. He deserves better than that
from Nathan.'

'Yes, he does. Frankly, Gemma, everyone deserves better than they're getting from Nathan. Why you still love him
after what he's done amazes me. Keeping my identity from

you was despicable enough, but when I think how he . . .
he—'

'You promised not to speak of that again,' Gemma broke
in sharply. 'You know that Nathan was out of his head when
he did that. If I can forgive and forget, why can't you?'

Celeste pursed disapproving lips. 'I'm sorry, but I can't
abide a man perpetrating any violence against a woman, no
matter what the provocation. Still, I won't mention it again.
It's your life and I can see you're determined to try to save
your marriage.'

'And you promised to help me any way you could.'

'God knows why,' Celeste muttered.

Gemma reached out and gently touched her mother on
the wrist. 'Because you love me?' she said softly.

Celeste was stunned by the rush of maternal love that
flooded her heart, tears pricking her eyes. Blinking madly,
she nodded acknowledgement of this, squeezing her
daughter's hands before finding her voice. 'I suppose I'll
just have to take your word for it that Nathan is worth
fighting for and not the coldest, most cynical bastard I've
ever laid eyes on.'

'Lenore thinks he's worth it,' Gemma argued with a quiet
intensity. 'And she was married to him for twelve years.'

Celeste sighed. 'Whatever his faults, he certainly knows
how to inspire loyalty in his wives.'

'He's only had two!' Gemma protested.

'So far. If he divorces you as he says he's going to, that
leaves the field clear for number three.'

'Nathan and I won't be getting a divorce,' Gemma said
with a stubborn set of her mouth. 'And there won't be any
number three!'

'Oh? And how do you intend to change his mind?'

'By whatever means are at my disposal.'

'Mmm . . .' Celeste gave Gemma the once-over, a sardonic gleam coming into her eyes as they carefully assessed
her appearance. 'I was at a loss earlier on to understand
what you hoped to achieve coming here tonight. Now I see
it's not your attending the play you had in mind but the
party afterwards.'

Gemma felt a guilty heat seep into her cheeks but she refused to succumb to embarrassment over her appearance, or shame over her plan. Nathan was her husband, after all! Besides, she wasn't nearly as provocatively dressed as she'd seen Celeste on occasions. OK, so her red crêpe dress was very form-fitting, the wide beaded belt emphasising her hour-glass figure. And yes, the deep V neckline showed clearly that she wasn't wearing a bra. But that was hardly a crime these days, was it?

'I only want to talk to him,' she lied outrageously. 'I can't achieve anything unless I talk to him, can I?'

'People who play with fire often get burnt,' Celeste warned softly. 'I should know. I've been there, done that.'

'And you ended up with the man you love, I noticed,' Gemma said. 'I aim to do the same.'

Celeste blinked in surprise at the hard edge in her daughter's voice, till it came to her that Gemma was a chip off the old block. Both her parents were pigheaded people who didn't know when to quit. She almost felt sorry for Nathan.

'Ah…here's Byron now.' Celeste smiled and linked arms with him. 'We thought you'd got lost, darling. How are things backstage?'

'Everyone's a bundle of nerves. Except Nathan, of course. That man had nerves of steel.'

And a heart of steel, Celeste thought, but declined to say so.

'What did he say about me?' Gemma asked nervously.

'Not a word.'

Gemma looked and felt crestfallen. 'Does…does he know I'm here, and that I'm going to the party afterwards?'

'I did mention it in passing, but he didn't seem to care one way or the other. To be honest, I'm a little shocked at Nathan's stand over this divorce business. I've never known him to be so inflexible, or so unfeeling. It's as though he's retreated behind some hard shell that nothing can penetrate.'

'That's just a façade he hides behind,' Gemma stated, and did her best to believe it. Because if she didn't, what then?

'It's time we went inside, isn't it?' Celeste jumped in, deciding a change of subject was called for when she saw a stricken look momentarily flash across her daughter's eyes. God, if that bastard hurt her again, she was going to kill him with her bare hands, something she was capable of. All those years of martial arts training had to be good for something!

'The bell hasn't gone,' Byron replied. 'But yes,' he added quickly on seeing Celeste's withering glance, 'I think we might go in.'

A photographer snapped the three of them as they walked into the theatre, Celeste and Byron flashing him a quick smile. Gemma's face, however, reflected an inner misery that she could not hide. Her faith in her plan was already crumbling, as was her faith in Nathan's love for her.

Their seats were in the middle of the fifth row from the front, the best seats in the house. As the play's producer, Byron had access to this whole row if he wanted. He'd offered seats to both Jade and Ava, but they had declined to come in protest over Nathan's unreasonable behaviour towards Gemma. Both women had declared they would never speak to him again till he came to his senses.

Gemma sat down and began flicking through the programme booklet Byron had bought her on arrival, anything to still the butterflies in her stomach. The sight of her husband's face staring out at her jolted her for a second.

The black and white photograph brought a hardness to his looks that she had never noticed before. He'd always looked like a golden god to her, with hair the colour of wheat, skin like bronze satin, a classically handsome face, a highly sensual mouth and the most beautiful grey eyes. Now, those eyes stared out at her with all the warmth of a winter's dawn, a slight arching of his left eyebrow adding a cynical edge to their cold expression, as did the twisted curve of his half-smile.

Oh, how she'd always hated it when he smiled at her like that, as though he knew things about the world that she was not yet privy to. Nathan had always declared the world a rotten place full of rotten people. He was cynical through and through about the human race, and the female sex in particular, probably because of the wicked, even depraved women who had played vital roles during his growing-up years.

First there had been his mother, a spoiled rich bitch who had left home as a teenager to live a life of debauchery, drugs and total self-indulgence. Nathan had been illegitimate, his father unknown to him and possibly to his mother, who had spent her entire life going from lover to lover, orgy to orgy, trip to trip.

Gemma had heard about Nathan's mother from several sources—though not Nathan himself. He never talked about the past. Apparently, she had put him in his first boarding-school at the age of eight, dragging him out whenever her latest lover left her or vice versa, then putting him back in school once a new man came on the scene. After she died of a drug overdose when Nathan was sixteen, he had become a street kid up at King's Cross. When Byron had come across him several months later Nathan had actually been living with some woman old enough to be his mother, and there was nothing platonic about the relationship. Byron had befriended the boy and, later, adopted him.

Gemma shuddered to think what might have happened to Nathan if Byron hadn't come along.

Not that Nathan's life as Byron's adopted son had ever been without its problems, especially when it came to the opposite sex. His relationship with the female members of his adoptive family seemed dicey from what she'd gathered, and his shotgun marriage to Lenore had not been a raving success, even if his plays were. By the time Gemma had met Nathan early this year when he was out at Lightning Ridge on an opal-buying trip, he'd become a rather world-weary thirty-five, divorced from Lenore and about to resign from Whitmore Opals to write full-time.

From the first moment they met, Gemma had been totally smitten by his mature handsomeness, his city glamour and smooth sophistication, while Nathan had seemed equally bowled over by her youthful beauty, countrified innocence and obvious inexperience with men. Gemma had initially been very wary of having anything to do with a divorced man so many years older than herself, but within a few short weeks of her coming to Sydney Nathan had seduced and married her.

Gemma had gone off on her honeymoon with many warnings about Nathan ringing in her ears. Not too many people had been confident that their marriage would work out, their view being that Nathan had only married her for the sex.

They'd been right and they'd been wrong. Sex had played a big part in their relationship so far. This did not bother Gemma as much as Nathan's jealous possessiveness, plus his tendency to treat her as a naïve child. His extreme cynicism was another bone of contention between them, along with his obvious inability to communicate with women on any other level than the physical.

But none of that meant he didn't really love her, Gemma kept believing staunchly. He just didn't know how to express that love any other way, or how to trust in it. Gemma believed that time would bring about the real intimacy and bonding she was looking for with Nathan. Time and love. She had no intention of giving up on her marriage at the first hurdle.

OK, so it was a pretty stiff hurdle. Not many wives would forgive their husbands falsely accusing them of unfaithfulness and then virtually raping them. But Gemma had, after all, been the first to point the finger in the matter of unfaithfulness. As for the rape...she understood why and how that had happened, and with the understanding had come forgiveness.

Nathan had gone crazy when he'd found her in Damian Campbell's bedroom. Fury had turned to a violent passion which had spun out of control before he could stop himself. Maybe if she had struggled instead of lying there in stunned horror, Nathan might have stopped. As it was, his remorse afterwards had been a palpable thing, and while Gemma had been shocked and appalled at first, in the end she'd been able to put the unfortunate incident into perspective.

Which was just as well, since it was possible Nathan had started a baby in her that afternoon. He'd obviously forgotten that he'd asked her to throw away her pills the previous weekend. But throw them away she had.

Most women might have revolted at a rape making them pregnant. But once Gemma had found it in her heart to forgive Nathan, she'd been consumed by an amazing feeling of rightness. It had also given her a way of getting her husband back. Hadn't he married Lenore—a woman he hadn't loved—on the strength of a pregnancy? Surely he'd come back to a wife he already loved if she was having his baby.

Which was why she was going to the post-première party tonight, hoping for an opportunity to seduce her husband, thereby increasing her chance of pregnancy, and at the same time freeing Nathan from having to accept that any baby she might have already conceived had been started on that awful afternoon. Gemma might have forgiven Nathan for the rape but it was clear to her that he hadn't forgiven himself. She was sure this was one of the reasons he was insisting on a divorce, because of his own self-disgust and guilt.

'It's not a very good photo of Lenore, is it?' Celeste suddenly commented, looking over Gemma's shoulder at the page across from the one she'd been staring blankly at.

Gemma refocused on the booklet in her lap and examined the photograph of the woman who was not only Nathan's ex-wife but also the leading lady in his new play.

Celeste was quite right. It was not a particularly flattering photo, though once again the black and white print did not do justice to Lenore's vivid beauty. In colour and in the flesh, Lenore was strikingly lovely, her bright red hair and flashing green eyes projecting a 'look-at-me' quality which no doubt served her well as a stage actress. Gemma imagined that from the moment Lenore walked on stage, all eyes would turn to her as though magnetised.

Though going on thirty-five, Lenore looked much younger, her figure still as spectacular as her face, its model-slim tallness and elegance adding to her already captivating package. Gemma had always felt gauche by comparison. No matter how many people complimented her pretty face and eyes, no matter how many men ogled her voluptuous curves, Gemma only had to look at Nathan's wife to feel inadequate and inferior.

Lenore's stunning sex appeal was the main reason Gemma had been so quick to believe what she had believed last Sunday, which was that Nathan had spent the weekend with his ex-wife while she'd been out at Lightning Ridge trying to find some clues to her till-then missing mother's identity. When Gemma had come back unexpectedly early and found Lenore in their flat with Nathan, she'd been right and ready to misunderstand tragically the seemingly shocking conversation she had overheard.

If she'd had a little more faith in her husband's love, she would have stayed and found out that they'd been rehearsing a section of their play, not discussing their previous night's dalliance. Instead, Gemma had fled, eventually to the Campbell house, thereby putting into motion the awful circumstances that had led to Nathan assaulting her.

The only good thing to come out of the horrors of the past week was that she not only found out her mother's identity, but had discovered, with a degree of relief, that the man who she had thought had been her father all her life and whom she had never been able to love was not her father after all!

'Byron tells me Lenore is having an affair with Zachary Marsden,' Celeste whispered. 'Apparently, they intend to marry next year after he's divorced his wife.'

'Yes, I know.'

'She's no danger to your marriage, Gemma.'

'Yes, I know that too. *Now*.'

'Better late than never.'

Gemma smiled across at her mother. 'Is that how you feel about marrying Byron?'

Celeste grinned. 'You'd better believe it. I can't wait to hog-tie him to me forever.'

'When's the big day?'

'As soon as we can arrange it. No long white dresses or anything. Just a simple ceremony. I have no patience with frippery at my age. All I want is Byron's ring on my finger.'

'And all I want is my Nathan back again.'

Celeste sighed. 'Are you sure your love for this man is not blind, Gemma? Do you know what you're dealing with? You were very young when you married him. Just twenty. You're only a few months older now.'

'You were only seventeen when you fell in love with Byron.'

Celeste shook her head. 'That's different.'

'How?'

'Will you two women stop whispering together?' Byron hissed down the line. 'The curtain's about to go up.'

Celeste patted his arm. 'Keep your shirt on, darling.'

'It's my shirt I'm worried about,' he grumbled back. 'I've put a hell of a lot of money into this play.'

'Don't worry, if it bombs I'll sell my yacht and give you the proceeds.'

'I just might keep you to that!'

'Sssh,' someone in the row behind them said as the lights dimmed and the curtain rose.

It wasn't long before everyone was silent and totally engrossed in what was going on on stage.

Gemma soon realised why the play was called *The Woman in Black*. The heroine, played by Lenore, was a widow in her mid-thirties, whose elderly husband had just died. Her wickedly handsome black-sheep stepson showed up at the funeral and immediately created an atmosphere of tingling suspense and sexual tension. It quickly became obvious that he had once had an affair with his stepmother and the affair had resulted in the birth of a son who the dead husband believed was his and who was now heir to the bulk of his estate.

Towards the end of the first half of the play the widow was once again in danger of being seduced by her evil stepson. He came to her bedroom the night after the funeral, where by some very devious and seductive manoeuvres he succeeded in binding her hand and foot to the bed. He was about to cut her nightwear off with a pair of scissors when the curtain came down.

'Good God,' Celeste let out on a shuddering sigh as the lights came on. Slowly, she turned wide eyes towards Gemma. 'And the man who wrote that is the man you *love*?'

Gemma flushed fiercely. 'It's only a play, Celeste. It's not real!'

'Still...'

'My God, I'm on a winner!' Byron exclaimed excitedly. 'Just look at the audience. They can't stop talking about it. I knew when I first read the darned thing that it was a powerfully emotional and erotic drama, but to see it enacted...' He shook his head in disbelief and admiration. 'Lenore's quite brilliant, isn't she? And that chap they've got playing the hero is simply incredible!'

'He's hardly a hero, Byron,' Celeste remarked drily.

'You know what I mean. Besides, I'll bet there isn't a woman in this theatre who'd say no to him if he put his slippers under her bed.'

'You could be right,' she said, revelling in the look of instant jealousy that burnt in his intense blue eyes.

'In that case, I'm not taking *you* to the party afterwards. That devil will be there. Gemma can go alone!'

'I doubt she'll mind that,' Celeste muttered, thinking Gemma might not want her father to see what she was up to. Despite Byron's passionate nature, he was basically a man of old-fashioned principles. It was the man's place to do the chasing, in his opinion, not the woman's. Seduction was not supposed to be a woman's domain. He was still coming to terms with Celeste's liberated views and would not condone his daughter doing her darnedest to get her husband back in her bed by the methods she obviously meant to employ later tonight. Celeste decided it might be wise to coax Byron away from the party afterwards as early as possible.

She didn't think she would have any trouble.

Her hand came to rest with seeming innocence on his thigh. 'Don't be silly, Byron,' she said, her eyes locking on his. 'You'll be expected to attend. At least for a little while,' she added, dropping her voice to a husky whisper, her hand moving ever so slightly up his leg. 'But I see no reason why we can't slip away early. If Gemma wants to stay and talk to Nathan she can go home to Belleview in a taxi.'

'You're wicked,' he groaned, but did not remove her hand.

She simply smiled. The things a mother did for her children, Celeste thought with a stab of perverse amusement.

Byron cleared his throat. 'Can I—er—get you two ladies a drink?' he offered, his voice a little shaky.

'That would be nice, darling,' Celeste returned smoothly. 'Champagne, I think. Celebrations are obviously in order.'

'Champagne it is.'

'What are we celebrating?' Gemma asked after Byron left them. Clearly, she hadn't been listening to their ongoing conversation.

'The success of the play.'

Gemma grimaced. 'I suppose I should be happy for Nathan, but I'll never like that play. How can I when it was responsible for breaking up our marriage?'

'The play wasn't responsible for breaking up your marriage. Nathan was, when he refused to listen to you, when he closed his eyes and ears to your love.'

Gemma frowned as the reality of what Celeste was saying sank in. Why had Nathan turned his back on her love? Why? His blunt confession to having kept her in the dark about Celeste being her mother had been a deliberate act to drive her away and make her agree to a divorce. Would a man genuinely in love do that?

Her highly practical and logical brain reached for an answer but her heart didn't like the one it came up with. Nathan couldn't love her, in that case. Maybe he never had. Maybe everyone else was right and he'd only married her out of lust. Maybe he'd even found someone else . . . the number three Celeste had mentioned.

Panic began to set in till Gemma remembered the baby she might be carrying. Could she afford to think negative thoughts, even if they were logical ones? Love wasn't logical, she reminded herself frantically. Love had never been logical. Perhaps it was shame and guilt that had impelled him to push her away with the only weapon he could find. That report. He *did* love her. He must! For if he didn't...

God, if he *didn't*!

Black thoughts swirled in her head.

'You don't *have* to go to the party afterwards,' Celeste said quietly.

Gemma blinked, her confusion clearing as she realised that if there was even the smallest chance Nathan loved her she had to take it.

'Oh, yes, I do,' she said, her nerves calming a little in the face of having no alternative. 'I don't have any choice.'

Celeste almost argued with her daughter, till she recalled all the stupid, crazy things she had done in the name of love. Could anyone have dissuaded her at the time? She doubted it.

So she remained silent, and eventually Byron returned with the champagne. Eventually, too, the play resumed, the second half as compelling and shocking as the first. And eventually, the three of them left the theatre to go to the post-première party.

CHAPTER TWO

'WHY didn't you hold this party at Belleview?' Celeste asked Byron as he drove up the ramp of the underground car park. 'Not that I'm complaining, mind. Double Bay is a lot closer than St Ives.'

'Which is precisely the answer to your question. The cast and crew have two performances tomorrow, it being a Saturday, and most of them live close to the city. So when Cliff offered his place as the venue I jumped at it.'

'Who's Cliff? One of your business cronies?'

'He'd like to be. He's an American movie producer who wants to buy the rights to Nathan's play. A colleague of his snapped one up earlier in the year. When Cliff read it, he hot-footed it over here as if he was shot out of a cannon. He's as slick as they come and thinks we Aussies have all come down in the last shower when it comes to the movie business. Which we have, in a way,' Byron finished drily.

'Don't let him have the rights to this play for less than two million, Byron,' Celeste advised. 'I've heard that's what a top screenplay commands these days.'

'Two million, eh? You're sure that's not excessive?'

'Not at all. That play will be a big hit, be it on stage or screen.'

'You're right!' Byron pronounced firmly. 'It's easily worth two million. I'll ask for three.'

'That's the spirit,' Celeste laughed.

Gemma sat silently in the back of Byron's Jaguar, grateful for her parents' lively conversation. It took her mind off the evening ahead, and her mission impossible. She wondered idly what kind of place this American movie mogul had rented. A large harbour-side apartment, she supposed. A penthouse, even.

When Byron turned down a quiet Double Bay street and pulled into the kerb outside an outlandishly huge Mediterranean-style white-stuccoed mansion, her eyes almost popped out of her head. She would not have believed that any home could make Belleview pale by comparison, but she was wrong. This particular place dwarfed Byron's home in size, outdid it for opulence, and made her realise that, while money could not buy everything, it could buy a hell of a lot!

Celeste must have been having similar thoughts.

'If he can afford a place like this, Byron,' she said as they climbed out of the car, 'then three million will be just a drop in the ocean.'

A security guard checked their identities at the gates, then let them inside.

Gemma was all eyes as they made their way through the lushly tropical front garden—complete with fountain—up some statue-lined steps and on to an arched portico that was at least twenty feet wide and God knew how long. It disappeared into the dim distance as did the ranch-style building itself. The ceramic pots lining the covered veranda at regular intervals were enormous and alone would have cost a small fortune.

Byron moved over to ring the front doorbell while Gemma turned to admire the gushing fountain from the top of the steps.

'If only Ma could see this place,' she muttered.

'Have you told Ma about me yet?' Celeste asked her daughter on hearing her mention her old neighbour out at Lightning Ridge.

Gemma nodded. 'I wrote to her last night. She's going to be tickled pink when she finds out Byron is my father. I think she always rather fancied him.'

'Did she, now?' Celeste said archly. 'I think I'll have to put a stop to all those opal-buying trips dear Byron goes on. I've never subscribed to the theory that absence makes the heart grow fonder. I'm more inclined to believe out of sight out of mind, especially where the male sex is concerned!'

Gemma laughed. 'Ma's about seventy, Celeste. I don't think you have to worry on that score.'

'Worry?' Byron butted in. 'What are you worried about, Gemma? Look, I'm sure Nathan will come round eventually. Give the boy some time and he'll see sense.'

Byron's reminder of why she had come to this party brought a resurgence of nerves to Gemma's stomach. Her confidence slipped another notch and it took all of her courage not to turn and run away.

'Nathan is not a boy, Byron,' Celeste advised tartly. 'And we weren't talking about him, anyway. Did you ring the doorbell?'

Right at that moment, the heavy front door was flung open and a big, barrel-chested man with a ruddy face and thick white hair appeared, a glass of whisky in one hand and a cigar in the other.

'Byron, my man!' he boomed in a broad American accent. 'I've been waiting for you to show up. Everyone else has been here for a while. What kept you?'

'The Press.'

Cliff laughed. 'I saw them swarming all over you afterwards. I gather they were keen on the play?'

'Very keen.'

'How could they not be?' the American enthused. 'The damned thing was brilliant! If you don't sell me the rights, I'll have to throw myself off your Gap.'

Gemma was startled by this mention of a rather notorious Sydney suicide spot since she hadn't really been tuned into the interchange. Her mind had been elsewhere.

Byron merely laughed. 'That's a bit drastic. I'm sure we could be persuaded to sell at the right price. Have you a spare three million or so?'

'Three million! Why, you Aussie rogue, you! But let's not talk money matters on the front doorstep. I'm much better at negotiation after a pint or two of Southern Comfort. And with a bit of luck, you won't be,' he chuckled.

'Come in, ladies, come in,' Cliff continued expansively, and threw an appreciative glance first at Celeste, then at Gemma. '*Two* women, Byron?' he joked as he ushered the threesome into the spacious terracotta-tiled foyer. 'I thought you were a conservative widower. Is this a side to you I haven't seen before?'

Byron gave him a look of mock horror. 'Good lord, Cliff, one woman is enough for me to handle, especially one like this.' He linked arms with Celeste and drew her forward. 'Let me introduce my fiancée, Celeste Campbell. Celeste, this is Cliff Overton.'

Celeste shook his hand and smiled with mischievous seductiveness.

Cliff whistled. 'I see what you mean, Byron. And who's this gorgeous young thing?' he said on turning to Gemma. 'I don't recall seeing you on stage tonight, honey, yet someone as lovely-looking as you are must surely be an actress. I could set up a screen test for you, if you like,' he whispered conspiratorially.

'Back off, Cliff,' Byron said, putting a protective arm around Gemma's shoulder. 'Gemma doesn't want to be an actress, do you, love?'

'Gemma! What a fantastic stage name!' Cliff gushed on before Gemma could get a word in edgeways. 'And so individual. All it needs is the right surname. I can see it in lights now. GEMMA STONE.'

Celeste and Gemma rolled their eyes at each other while Byron's mouth thinned. 'Gemma is Nathan's wife,' he informed drily. 'I doubt he would like to see her name in lights.'

The American's broad grin faded to a puzzled frown. 'She *is*? But I thought Nathan was divorced. I mean, he—er—well, never mind,' he shrugged. 'I must have got it wrong. Nice to meet you, Gemma. You must be very proud of that genius husband of yours. That is *some* play he's written. Not to mention directed. I wonder if he'd consider coming to Hollywood to direct the movie. What do you think, Byron?'

'You'll have to ask Nathan that. He's his own man. I presume he's here?'

Their host looked oddly disconcerted again. 'Er—yes... yes, he is. Somewhere...'

'Perhaps we could go and find him, then?' Byron suggested, and Gemma's stomach clenched down hard. Suddenly, she didn't want to see Nathan. Not here. Not with a lot of other people around. She'd been stupid to come.

Her spirits sinking with each step, she followed the others down the wide tiled corridor to find herself eventually standing in an archway that overlooked a huge sunken living area full of laughing, talking, drinking, smoking partygoers. Music played in the background though only one couple was dancing. Lively conversation and thin cigarette haze filled the air.

The first person Gemma spotted was Lenore, who was standing, arm in arm with her leading man, surrounded by a rather large group of people. Everyone was drinking champagne and generally looking very happy and excited. When Lenore spotted Gemma too, her first reaction was a worried frown and a darting glance down the other end of the room. Gemma's eyes followed, and what she saw made her breath catch in her throat and her insides flip right over.

Nathan was sitting on a large padded leather sofa. And the beautiful blonde curled up next to him was hardly acting like a platonic acquaintance. She was all over him like a rash and Nathan wasn't warding her off.

Gemma's mouth went dry as she watched her husband bend forward to pick up a drink from the table in front of them, laughing and smiling with his companion as they shared the glass. When he brushed his companion's hair with his lips Gemma was almost sick on the spot. Suddenly, he looked up over the blonde's head, straight at the archway then straight into Gemma's appalled face. Without acknowledging her, he looked away and started talking to the couple seated on an adjacent sofa, his arm still firmly around the blonde's shoulder.

'Who the hell is that with Nathan?' Celeste snapped from where she was standing between Gemma and Byron.

'Her name is Jody Something-or-other,' Byron grated out. 'She's one of the understudies.'

'I'd hoped I got the wrong idea earlier,' Cliff muttered on the other side of Byron. 'Clearly I hadn't.'

'Gemma, darling,' Celeste said abruptly, grabbing her daughter by the shoulders and dragging her back out of sight. 'Why don't I take you home? You can see for yourself Nathan doesn't want a reconciliation. Don't belittle yourself by trying. *Please.*'

Having snapped out of her shocked reaction, Gemma's logical brain jolted into gear. What she'd seen with her eyes didn't make sense. Nathan loved *her*, not some strange woman. In that case, what was he doing, draped all over her like that and doing something as intimate as sharing a drink, not to mention kissing her hair?

Every instinct told her to flee. But she'd run away once before when things looked bad and look what had happened!

'I . . . I *have* to talk to him.'

'Not in there, for pity's sake,' Celeste said, nodding towards the crowded and quite noisy room. She turned to her host, her voice assertive. 'Cliff, you must have a quiet room near by where Gemma could speak privately with Nathan.'

'Yes, of course!'

Gemma was ushered back down the corridor and through a door into a darkly furnished study-cum-library, where she waited with Celeste while Byron went to get Nathan. A lingering nausea continued to swim in her stomach as she tried desperately to get a grasp on the situation. But it was beyond her.

Nathan came in the room alone, looking elegantly cool in his black dinner suit, not the slightest bit perturbed at having to face his estranged wife.

'You wanted to see me, Gemma?' he drawled with an indifference that stunned her.

'You unfeeling bastard,' Celeste bit out. 'We saw you just now with that little tramp.'

Icy grey eyes turned her way. 'Watch your mouth, Celeste. Jody is no tramp. And I should know. I've seen plenty of the real thing. I'm looking at one right now.'

'Nathan!' Gemma gasped, appalled by such open rudeness.

'It's all right, Gemma,' Celeste said sharply. 'I can take care of myself. Now you listen to me, you creep! For some weird and wonderful reason which eludes me, Gemma here still loves you, and believes you still love her. Or she did till she saw that lovely little scenario out there with that blonde! But you and I know what you are, don't we? You're not fit to be the husband of a lovely young girl like this. Why don't you do her a favour? Get the hell out of her life and stay out of it!'

'Celeste, please,' Gemma groaned, clasping her hands to the sides of her head.

'I'd like to do exactly that, Celeste,' Nathan snarled. 'Your precious daughter just isn't getting the message. Why in God's name you allowed her to come here tonight is beyond me. I don't want her back. I want a divorce. What more is there to be said?'

'There's plenty more to be said!' Gemma suddenly burst out. 'And I want it said to *me*! I'm here in this room, Nathan. Don't talk around me.'

He turned slowly to face her, the cold fury in his eyes making her flinch away. 'I have nothing more to say to you.'

Gemma almost crumbled at that point, but she knew if she walked out of here right now without asking him critical questions, she would never be able to live with herself, or the doubts that would remain. 'But I have things I want to say to *you*, Nathan,' she said with more steel than she was actually feeling.

His shrug was indifferent. 'Please yourself.'

Gemma turned to her mother. 'Celeste? Will you leave me alone with Nathan?'

Celeste grimaced. 'I don't like this, but I suppose I have no alternative. It is your life, after all. I'll join Byron for a while. But I won't be far away.'

Giving Nathan a warning glance, Celeste strode from the room, banging the door shut behind her. A strained silence descended, with Gemma eventually moving a little nervously away from Nathan.

'You don't have to do that,' he snapped. 'I'm not going to attack you again.'

'Good God, Nathan,' she groaned, 'is that what all this is really about? Do you think that I can't possibly have forgiven you for what you did that day? I can and I do, because I understand the pressures you were under when you did it.'

'You misunderstand me, Gemma,' he returned coldly. 'I do not care if you forgive me or not. And it's immaterial to me now whether you slept with Campbell or not.'

'But I didn't! I swear to you, I didn't. I won't deny that he fancied me and that he might have wanted something to develop between us. But nothing did. And now that he's found out he's my uncle, there's no risk of that.'

Nathan's laughter sent a chill running through her soul. 'As if something as trivial as a little incest would stop a man like that. God, but you still haven't grown up, have you? I would have thought some time spent in the bosom of the Campbells would have opened up those innocent eyes of yours.'

Gemma closed those eyes with a pained sigh before opening them again, her expression sad as she surveyed her cynical husband. 'You always believe the worst of people, don't you? Not everyone is wicked, Nathan.'

He laughed, then moved slowly towards her, making Gemma stiffen inside with an odd mixture of excitement and apprehension. When he reached out, to tip her chin upwards with a single finger, her eyes were wide and fearful.

'If they aren't, my darling,' he said in a dark silky voice, 'then it's only a question of time and opportunity. Even the best person can be corrupted, given the right weapons. Just look at Byron. All he needed was a woman like Celeste to come into his life and his morals went right out of the window. With some people it's sex. With others it's drugs. Or money. Or power. Total innocents can be corrupted even against their will, if they fall into the wrong hands.'

The awfulness of Nathan's words seemed to get lost under the spell of his physical closeness, and that finger which had slid under her chin and was even now tracing an erotic circle around her quivering mouth. Smoky grey eyes locked on to hers and Gemma found herself unable to tear her gaze away from his.

'I could have really corrupted you if I'd wanted to,' he murmured thickly.

Gemma moaned softly when that tantalising finger retreated from those tortuous circles. Dazed, she just stood there for a moment till she realised he was staring down at her braless breasts, which were at that moment rising and falling with a betrayingly increased heartbeat.

'Maybe I already have,' he rasped, startling her when he slipped his hands into the deep neckline and slid the dress off her shoulders, dragging the material down her arms, till her breasts were totally exposed.

'Why else would you have dressed like this tonight?' he taunted, his thumbs rubbing her rapidly hardening nipples. 'Unless you wanted me to see that your breasts were within easy reach. Unless you wanted me to touch them like this, maybe touch you far more intimately...'

She whimpered as desire shot through her, her heart leaping when his eyes locked on to hers and she saw an answering desire flare madly within his glittering gaze.

'If I did,' she whispered breathlessly, 'it's because I love you. And because I know you still love me.'

Her words brought a stunned look to his face, quickly followed by a darkening fury.

'Then you're a bloody fool!' he exclaimed, angrily yanking her dress back into place. 'I do not love you and neither do you love me. God, there I was, thinking you might have grown up a little, that you might have learnt to call our feelings for each other by its correct name. It's called lust, Gemma. L-U-S-T. Only romantic-minded little fools talk of love when they mean sex. Now get out of here before I do something we're both going to regret afterwards.'

Gemma stared up at him with her mouth agape and her head whirling.

'Didn't you hear me, you silly little bitch?' he snarled. 'Get out! And take your naïveté with you. I have no patience with it any more. I should never have damned well married you in the first place and nothing you or anyone else can say will stop me divorcing you!'

Gemma stumbled over to the door where she gripped on to the knob with a white-knuckled intensity. But she did not turn that knob. She dragged some deep, steadying breaths and, when she felt enough in control, slowly turned to face her husband once more.

'Just tell me one thing before I go,' she said.

'What?' he snapped, scowling over at her.

'If you never loved me, and didn't believe I loved you, then why *did* you marry me? You could have had me without marrying me. You *did* have me without marrying me!'

His sardonic laugh increased her confusion, and her pain. 'So I did. And you were enchanting, my dear. So enchanting that I thought I wanted you in my bed for forever and exclusively. I was even prepared to let you have a child to keep you there. Foolish of me, I realise. But even a mature man can be made a fool of when in the grip of a sexual obsession. Frankly, I was still quite enamoured of your charms when fate stepped in and sent you racing off to Campbell Court, which is why I reacted so poorly to finding you in Damian Campbell's bedroom.'

'But I wasn't sleeping in there!' she cried. 'How many times do I have to tell you that I never went to bed with Damian?'

'As I said before, dear heart,' Nathan drawled, 'I no longer care whether you did or not. My maniacal appetite for youth and innocence seems to have been cured somewhere along the line. Perhaps you saw the cure yourself with me earlier? She's thirty-three, blonde and very, very inventive.'

Gemma stared at him before shaking her head in a blank and bleak disbelief. 'I never really knew you, did I?' she said dazedly. 'Damian did. He said you were bad. I should have believed him.'

Angry grey eyes snapped back to hers. 'Why didn't you, then?'

'Because I stupidly believed you loved me,' she countered, her agony switching to outrage. 'I stupidly believed in *you*!'

'Yes, that was stupid, I'll grant you that.'

Gemma could only keep shaking her head at him. 'You don't have any conscience at all where women are concerned, do you? You're like that hero in your play. Sex and lust are all there is for you. You probably *did* sleep with Irene as Damian said you did.'

Nathan smiled a smile that sent a shiver down Gemma's spine.

'You know, some day that bastard is going to get his just deserts.'

'I suppose you're going to say he's lying about that as well,' she said bitterly.

'Not if agreeing I went to bed with Irene will get you out of that door and out of my life.'

Gemma blinked her shock.

'Oh, for God's sake,' he swept on irritably. 'Of course I didn't sleep with that pathetic bitch. Give me some credit for taste! But I dare say you won't believe me. If you did, that would mean your precious uncle must have lied to you.'

'I...I suppose Irene could have lied to him about it,' Gemma said hesitatingly.

'Good thinking, Gemma,' he praised, but in a mocking tone. 'Amazing how one and one doesn't always make two, isn't it? Sometimes you have to look outside the dots.'

Gemma frowned. 'And should I look outside the dots with you, Nathan? Could you be driving me away because you think it's for my own good, that you're no good for me?'

His laughter was dark but not without humour. 'That's so splendidly noble, I wish I could embrace it! But that *would* be lying, my darling,' he said, walking towards her with such a wicked glitter in his eyes that she shrank back against the wall next to the door.

'Don't touch me,' she whispered.

Nathan's raised eyebrows were pure sarcasm. 'Don't touch you? A few minutes ago you were dying for me to touch you. What's happened to change that, I wonder? Are you beginning to doubt my sense of honour? Are you afraid that at any moment I might change into the animal of the other day?'

'I'm not afraid of you, Nathan,' she lied bravely.

'Then you should be,' he warned in a raw whisper. 'Because if you stay here any longer, Gemma, my sweet, I might set about really corrupting you, just for the hell of it!'

Gemma stared at him, appalled at this dark stranger who had been her husband but whom she did not know.

'Too late,' he mocked. 'I withdraw the offer. Besides, I just remembered I promised Jody a night of indefatigable energy. If I use some of it up on you, darling, I just won't have enough to go around.'

Gemma's hand came up and slapped him. His head jerked back and a red mark immediately stained his cheek, but he made no move to retaliate, merely rubbed his cheek and smiled a faintly wry smile. 'Feel better now?' he taunted softly.

'I hate and despise you, Nathan Whitmore,' Gemma rasped, her voice shaking. 'How you can look yourself in the mirror in the morning, I have no idea. I came here to this party tonight hoping that we could get back together again. I was prepared to forgive you everything because I thought you loved me, and because I loved you. But I don't love you any more. I refuse to love someone so unworthy of being loved.'

'You've no idea how pleased I am to hear that, Gemma. Because I don't want your love. It's the last thing I want from you.'

Gemma could no longer deny the harsh sincerity behind the chillingly delivered words. But oh, dear God...what was going to become of her...without Nathan...without her dreams...? What point was there in going on?

'So why are you still standing there?' he jeered. 'What more is there to be said? You're free, Gemma. Free of our marriage. Free of loving me. Free of *me*. I'd say you're one lucky girl, wouldn't you? Now leave me be,' he bit out savagely, and turned his back on her.

Gemma somehow made it out of the room and back to Celeste, who took one look at her and called for Byron to take them both home.

CHAPTER THREE

LIFE went on.

Gemma would not have believed it could after her traumatic meeting with Nathan. Surely she must die from the pain and the hurt that was consuming every fibre of her being? Nathan didn't love her; had never loved her. All her dreams and hopes for the future were obliterated by that one cruel admission. As for the past . . . it was almost as painful to look back as it was to look bleakly forward. Her marriage had been a mockery, doomed from the start. Why hadn't she heeded the signs? Why had she stubbornly refused to see what others saw?

Because you *are* a naïve silly bitch, that's why, an angry inner voice kept telling her. Or you *were*!

It was this angry inner voice that sustained her through the following day, refusing to let her break down totally, although there were frequent bouts of weeping, as well as long hours of deep depression. But in the end anger, plus a healthy dose of burgeoning bitterness, stopped Gemma from succumbing to total despair.

When she woke on Sunday to the news that Nathan had delivered her car during the night—complete with the rest of her belongings—leaving again without speaking to anyone, her sense of outrage knew no bounds. What had happened to the man she had first met and fallen in love with? Where was this wicked stranger coming from? Had he always been there, hiding behind that cool conservative façade, that seemingly decent persona? He must have been, she supposed, her bewilderment almost as great as her disillusionment.

Still, she wasn't the only one to be fooled. Byron had
clearly been taken in, as had Lenore. Ava and Melanie
however, had clearly had their misgivings about him al
along. Jade had been ambivalent, warning her off Nathan
at first before unexpectedly coming round to believe in hi
love for Gemma almost as much as she had.

But he hadn't been able to sustain the act indefinitely, had
he? His dark side had finally surfaced, and surfaced with a
vengeance. She now felt utterly mortified at having for
given him for the rape. He had probably enjoyed every per
verse moment, his supposed feelings of betrayed love being
nothing but a bruised ego that his sexual possession migh
have dared turn to another man.

By Sunday evening, Gemma found solace in a bitter de
termination not to fall apart over the bastard's black
treachery. He wasn't worth it. So on the Monday morning
she gritted her teeth and went back to work.

From the first moment she walked into the shop, Gemma
realised that the news of her separation from Nathan mus
have got around, because all the girls were extraordinarily
nice to her, which was something new.

When Byron had given her a job as a sales assistant in the
more exclusive of his two city stores, Gemma had gradually
noticed an underlying resentment from the rest of the staff
She supposed they thought her employment smacked o
nepotism, even though she had quickly proved herself a very
competent salesperson, her Japanese better than anyone
else's. Gemma believed she might have overcome her work
mates' underlying hostility if Nathan hadn't vetoed her go
ing out with them on social occasions.

In the circumstances, she didn't blame them for thinking
she was a snob, so she was quite touched by their kindness
to her that morning, and found it hard not to dissolve into
tears. With a stiff upper lip and a lot of false smiles, she
made it through the morning, but as one o'clock ap
proached Gemma couldn't wait to spend an hour sitting by
herself in a park somewhere.

At a couple of minutes past one she was walking through
the hotel arcade, heading for the main exit, her eyes on the

black and white tiled floor, when a man's voice suddenly spoke from just behind her right shoulder. 'Going my way, sweetheart?'

Gemma ground to a halt and spun round, her startled brown eyes quickly filling with reproach. 'Damian, you bad man. You shouldn't sneak up on a girl like that.'

'Sometimes it's the only way,' he returned drily. 'Some girls don't answer telephone calls.'

Gemma coloured guiltily. 'I'm sorry. I was going to ring you back, but I forgot. Truly. I...I was a bit of a mess over the weekend.'

'I can imagine. Celeste filled me in on what happened last Friday night. Which is why I was so startled when Ava told me on the phone this morning that you'd gone to work.'

'It seemed the best thing to do.'

'I couldn't agree more. I'm delighted to see you're determined not to be down-in-the-mouth and dreary. Life's too short to waste it mooning over bastards like Nathan Whitmore.'

Gemma's reaction was instant and quite absurd. She wanted to scream at Damian that he had no right to judge Nathan, that he knew nothing about him at all! Just in time, she controlled the quite irrational urge, recognising it as a hangover from what she had so very recently and stupidly believed in her husband and his love for her. 'Yes, well, I'd rather not talk about Nathan, if you don't mind,' she said instead.

'Your wish is my command.' Damian took her arm. 'What would you like to talk about over lunch?'

Gemma felt a reluctant smile pull at her mouth as she was masterfully propelled towards the street. 'Who said I was having lunch with you?'

'You don't *want* to have lunch with your poor old uncle?' he replied teasingly.

She laughed at this description of himself. Damian was only twenty-nine. He was also the epitome of 'tall dark and handsome', with the added elegance and style that being very wealthy provided. Most men would have looked good

in the suit Damian was wearing. He looked fantastic. And
he knew it.

'Lunch is fine,' she agreed. 'But as I said, a mutual
tongue-lashing of Nathan is out. I also don't want to hear
any sarcasm about Byron and Celeste being my parents.'

'Hey!' Damian put up his hands in mock defeat. 'What
do you think I am, an unfeeling monster? All I want is to
have lunch with my very beautiful niece who, by the way,
looks gorgeous with her hair up. You must wear it that way
to the party this Friday night.'

'P...party? What kind of party?' Damian's sweet flat-
tery had been unacceptable. His inviting her to a party made
her uncomfortable for some unaccountable reason. Were
Nathan's vile accusations about Damian still lingering at the
back of her mind? It seemed the only reasonable explana-
tion for her sudden unease. Or maybe her trust in the male
sex in general had received such an incredible blow that it
would be a long time before she could trust another man.

'Just a dance party, Gemma,' Damian explained with an
indulgent smile. 'They're very popular with young people.
A lot of my friends go to them. I thought it might make you
feel better to get out and about, dance a little and meet some
new people.'

It did sound innocent enough. And Damian *was* her uncle. Why was she hesitating?

'I...I'm not sure.'

'Hey, no sweat. You don't have to do anything you don't
want to do any more. You're your own boss now, remember? Just think about it and if you decide you need some
cheering up come Friday night give me a call.' Smiling, he
linked arms with her again. 'Now let's go to lunch before
your hour is up and we haven't had a thing to eat!'

Gemma did need cheering up by Friday night. Frankly, she
needed cheering up a lot earlier than that.

Work occupied her mind during the day, but come night-
time, Belleview was hardly a hive of distracting activity and
conversation. Byron, quite rightly, was spending a lot of
time with Celeste, courting her as he should have courted her

all those years ago. And Ava, God love her, either disappeared into her studio with Vince or went out with him. Knowing Ava's history, Gemma did not have the heart to spoil her fun at this glorious time in her life.

So Gemma pretended to be quite happy staying home alone watching television, saying she was tired after being on her feet all day. Yet all the while she was getting more and more depressed. By the time Damian telephoned her on the Thursday night, it didn't take much persuasion for her to say yes.

Damian hung up, not bothering to hide his devilish glee. No one could see him. Celeste had just left with dear old Byron, and Cora was out in the kitchen, clearing up after dinner.

'At last,' he muttered, and let his mind run free over how Friday night should pan out.

Sweet little Gemma would have no resistance at all to the drugs he would slip into her drinks. In the end, she would have no resistance to *him*.

Damian actually trembled with the anticipated pleasure of finally having her in his power. God, but he had waited months for this moment. Never had a woman possessed his brain and his body as much as Gemma had.

From the first moment he'd seen her at that ball he'd wanted her, wanted her with a want that had gradually become an obsession. Her being his niece didn't change a thing. If anything, it would add a delightfully perverse edge to the experience.

Damian made his way slowly back upstairs while his thoughts raced feverishly on.

He was going to have to be very careful the first time. He would have to seem to give her everything she was looking for, and obviously needing. Tenderness. Comfort. Love...

Later, when she was totally addicted to the mindless ecstasy that the drugs and he could give her, he would introduce her to more refined pleasures. It was amazing the pain a woman could endure—and even welcome—when she was high on the right cocktail.

He would have to video-tape everything, of course, once it got to that stage. Otherwise she might be tempted to tell someone after the drugs wore off. He couldn't have that.

Damian smiled. He might even make some money out of her. It wouldn't be the first time. Amazing how much women were prepared to pay rather than have tapes of their sexual exploits posted to their husbands or their families. They never breathed a word, either. Damian considered it was ironic that it was Nathan himself who had first given him the idea of taping sexual encounters to blackmail women. Poor old Irene . . .

In a way, it was a form of justice that Nathan's own wife be similarly blackmailed.

Not that justice ever really interested Damian. He had only one aim in life.

Pleasure.

Sheer unadulterated pleasure.

He could hardly wait for tomorrow night to come.

Byron didn't come home for dinner on the Friday night. He'd organised to meet Celeste after work for dinner in town and a night at the theatre. Ava and Vince went out for dinner as well, over to Vince's family. Which meant Gemma would be alone at Belleview when Damian came to pick her up at nine o'clock. She hadn't told anyone yet about the dance party, and now that she didn't have to she was relieved.

Gemma hadn't been looking forward to facing the frowns of disapproval. All the Whitmores thought very badly of Damian, yet in all honesty she had never seen any evidence to support his reputation as a wild and dissolute playboy. Any concerns she had ever had over the man had come from everyone around Belleview bad-mouthing him, as they had bad-mouthed Celeste. He was probably as innocent of any real wrongdoing as his sister had proved to be.

Nathan had been the chief castigator of both Campbells, yet it was Nathan who had proven to be the wicked one.

Still, it worried Gemma that she hadn't told Ava some white lie about going out somewhere. What if Ava came home before Gemma and found her bed empty? The poor darling would worry and Gemma didn't want that.

In the end, she decided to leave a note propped up on her pillow saying a friend from work had rung and she'd gone out to a party, and not to worry if she got home late. Byron had given her a set of keys to the house, as well as a remote control for the gates, so there was no trouble with letting herself in.

With that problem solved, Gemma set about having a relaxing bath, then getting herself ready. She had plenty of time—apparently these parties didn't start early. Neither were they dressy affairs. Damian had suggested she wear something casual. Jeans or a skirt and top would be fine.

Gemma's wardrobe was full of mostly classic or tailored garments but she did have a reddish-brown leather skirt which, when teamed with a simple cream silk shirt looked fairly casual. The colour also suited the auburn highlights the hairdresser regularly put into her shoulder-length brown hair. Remembering the compliment Damian had given her earlier in the week, she put it up as she had that day in a loose knot, with lots of wispy bits left around her face and neck. She put gold loops in her ears and a couple of gold chains round her neck. As it was night time, she wore a reasonable amount of make-up, high heels and perfume.

Gemma was ready and waiting, the gates open and her cream clutch bag in hand, when Damian drove in shortly before nine. His low wolf whistle when she opened the door unnerved her slightly, as did his words.

'God, you look great. I'll have to beat the men off with broomsticks.'

When Gemma frowned her immediate unease, Damian smiled reassuringly at her. 'Don't worry, love, you're with me. If we don't tell anyone I'm your uncle, they won't come anywhere near you. Damian's bird always has a hands-off sign on her.'

Gemma wasn't entirely reassured by this idea, and neither did she like others thinking they were boyfriend and girlfriend, but she could see the sense of it if she didn't want to ward off unwanted advances all night. The thought of dancing with perfectly strange men was suddenly anathema to her. Why had she ever agreed to come? She was not ready for this in any way, shape or form.

'Even if I went around telling everyone I was your uncle,' Damian added with an amused gleam in his eye, 'no one would believe me.'

He was right, Gemma conceded as she looked him over. He looked younger than his twenty-nine years, especially when dressed all in black, as he was tonight. Absolutely everything he had on was black, from his high-necked shirt and casual woollen trousers down to his socks and shoes. There was even an ebony ring flashing on one finger and a black-faced watch on his wrist. At least no one would stare at them together as they had often done at her and Nathan.

A jab of intense dismay made her stiffen for a moment. Why do I keep thinking of him? Why can't I forget him as he has obviously forgotten me?

You know why, taunted a dark inner voice, and Gemma's hand instinctively moved across her stomach. God, what if she *was* pregnant? She didn't want to be. Not now. Not any more. She wanted to forget Nathan, to put him right out of her mind for the rest of her life.

'Are you feeling all right, Gemma?' Damian asked with such a warm concern she felt terribly guilty. Her worry was probably all for nothing anyway. Her period would be along any day, once her cycle got back to normal.

'I'm fine,' she said with a quick smile. 'And you're quite right, Damian. We make a handsome couple.'

He smiled, radiating that dazzling charm which no doubt sent all the women's hearts fluttering. But Gemma knew her heart was unlikely to flutter again for a long time. Not that it had ever fluttered for Damian. Nathan's jealousy had been way off the mark, and quite wasted.

A sharp bitterness shot through Gemma as she thought of all she had suffered at Nathan's hands because of what his sick mind imagined was going on between her and Damian. In a weird kind of way, she almost wished there had been something between them to justify the treatment she had endured. There was nothing worse than being accused of something you hadn't done, nothing worse than being punished when you were innocent.

'Stop thinking about that bastard,' Damian said abruptly, sending her thoughts scattering when he curled his hand around her empty one and pulled her down the front steps.

Gemma found herself belted into the passenger seat of Damian's red Ferrari before she could say boo.

'Wait!' she cried out when he zoomed through the open gates and would have taken off before she had a chance to close them. He screeched on the brakes, darting her a frustrated look.

'I have to close the gates,' she explained patiently, whereupon he gave her a sighing smile.

'For a second there, I thought you'd changed your mind about coming.'

'Never,' she said, determined to dismiss Nathan from her mind for tonight. He didn't deserve thinking about. 'Where is this dance party, by the way?'

'At a pub in North Sydney. You won't know it. It's in the back streets and not the newest establishment around, but the music's great and the drinks are cheap.'

Gemma laughed. 'I wouldn't think you'd care much if the drinks were cheap or not.'

Damian flashed her a wicked grin. 'Watch the pennies and the pounds will look after themselves,' he quipped. 'Light me a cigarette, would you? They're on the dash there, and there's a lighter in my left trouser pocket. Can't get it myself. Must concentrate on the road. This traffic's hell.'

The traffic on the Pacific highway was indeed bad. Every man and his dog seemed to be heading for the city. Nevertheless, Gemma felt very uncomfortable doing something as intimate as fishing around in Damian's trouser pocket. Luckily, she found the lighter quickly and was soon placing a glowing cigarette between Damian's lips. Their eyes met briefly as she did so and Gemma quickly looked away. For there had been nothing platonic in the look Damian had just given her. It had been oddly intense.

Either that, or her imagination was getting the better of her. The latter seemed the most likely.

Damian had always been a perfect gentleman in her company. Always. Nathan's wicked warnings had put the fear of the devil into her, Gemma decided. Listening to scurrilous gossip about people was wrong. And listening to unfounded fears was wrong too. She resolved not to do it any more.

With this in mind Gemma turned a smiling face back towards Damian. 'It's really sweet of you to take me out like this. I really needed it. I was feeling awfully down.'

'I know, honey, I know,' he said kindly. 'Leave it to dear old Uncle Damian. He knows exactly what you need to cheer you up...'

CHAPTER FOUR

LUKE wouldn't normally have been seen dead at a dance party. At thirty, he considered himself too old for such goings-on. He'd briefly gone through a stage for a couple of years after finishing uni where he haunted clubs, pubs and discos every Friday and Saturday night, but those days were long gone. His life was Campbell Jewels now.

He'd only come here tonight as a favour to his mother. Apparently his kid sister, Mandy, had been coming here nearly every Friday night lately and his mother wanted him to check the place out. Luke thought she was being overprotective, since Mandy was twenty and a very sensible girl, but he'd promised to drop in and see for himself if there was anything to worry about.

He stood in a corner of the room, shaking his head at what was before his eyes. How had he ever enjoyed this kind of thing? The screechingly loud music was enough to give anyone an instant migraine. Add to this the garish lights flashing on and off, the heavy pall of smoke and the crush of a hundred sweaty gyrating bodies in an area where possibly fifty might comfortably have fitted, and you had a scene he found quite repulsive.

Still, Luke wasn't too old that he couldn't ·appreciate Mandy would quite like such an atmosphere, but he was perturbed by how open the drug use was. Nobody bothered to hide the pill-popping and marijuana-smoking. Luke had also seen a couple of suspicious-looking packages changing hands and quite a few empty syringes in the bins in the toilet block. He began to worry if Mandy made a habit of coming to this place she might end up not being so sensible.

So Luke stayed in the dimly lit corner and waited, hoping she would show up and he could have a brotherly word in her ear. But after a further half-hour's peering through the smoke haze Mandy still hadn't turned up. He was about to leave when his attention was suddenly captured by a man dressed in black, an exceptionally handsome man with slick black hair, wicked black eyes and flashing white teeth.

Luke was not at all surprised to see Damian Campbell in a place like this. Everyone around Campbell's knew of his reputation for decadent living. He liked to mix with a young fast crowd. He liked his women beautiful, and he didn't care if they were married.

The girl with Damian was certainly beautiful, and very married.

Luke recognised Gemma Whitmore from the photograph in last Sunday's paper of her attending the première to Nathan's Whitmore's latest play. She'd been snapped alongside Celeste and Nathan's adoptive father, Byron Whitmore.

Now Luke was an astute man. He'd long known about the feud between the Campbells and the Whitmores. But one didn't have to be too astute to have noticed that something was afoot between the two families. Celeste Campbell and Byron Whitmore were suddenly as thick as thieves. Yet while that old feud business seemed to have gone out of the window, Luke still didn't think this extended to Damian draping himself all over Nathan Whitmore's wife.

Luke smelled a rat. And there wasn't a bigger rat around Sydney than Damian Campbell.

Luke watched his antics with distaste. The man was a real sleaze-bag. Under the guise of dancing, he was touching Mrs Whitmore wherever he could, finally putting her arms around his neck then curving his hands over her buttocks, pulling her hard against him.

Suddenly, the girl wrenched away from him, swaying violently on her feet. The look on her face was one of total confusion. It was then that Luke realised she was under the influence of some drug or other. Alcohol was unlikely to produce that type of bewilderment. He decided to edge closer and see if he could pick up some of their conversation.

'I...I don't think I like it here, Damian,' the girl was saying in a very slurred voice. Her hand fluttered up to her forehead. 'I...I feel hot, and sort of funny. You'd better take me home.'

'I'll get you a cool drink first,' Damian offered, and led her over to a wall where he virtually propped her against it. 'Stay here. I won't be long.'

Luke didn't know what to do. He didn't want to tangle with Damian Campbell, especially not after just being given the job as sales and marketing manager at Campbell's. But Gemma Whitmore's reactions bothered him. Clearly, she wasn't sure what was going on. Luke suspected she hadn't knowingly taken drugs. If she had, she wouldn't be acting so confused over her condition.

With this thought in mind, Luke followed Damian to the bar and watched while the bastard slipped some powder into the orange juice, mixing it very well while his eyes darted slyly around. Damn, he was right! He was drugging that girl without her knowledge.

Yet it wasn't any of his business, was it?

For a full ten minutes Luke argued with his conscience, then, with a resigned sigh, went in search of trouble. But Damian and the girl were no longer on the dance-floor or anywhere in the room. Swearing at himself, Luke raced outside to the car park where he spotted Damian leaning Mrs Whitmore against a car and kissing her. The girl's arms were dangling limply by her sides, like a rag doll.

Luke felt fury well up inside him. He didn't stop to think any longer, didn't stop to count the cost of his actions, just charged across the car park, whirled Campbell away from the girl and socked him one right on the jaw.

No one was more surprised than Luke when Damian crumpled immediately, falling blessedly unconscious to the concrete. Luke didn't think he'd even seen what hit him. Or who.

'Hey!' some bloke called out from a few cars away. 'What's going on there?'

Luke didn't stay around for any explanations. He swooped up the girl from where she had slid down to sit blank-eyed on the ground, and virtually carried her over to where his own car was parked. Stuffing her into the passenger seat, he raced around to get in and screeched away before anyone could collar him. He wasn't sure what he was going to do, especially after a glimpse in the rear-view mirror showed Damian Campbell getting groggily to his feet.

It was only after he'd driven several blocks and felt secure that no one was following that he pulled over to the kerb and tried to assess the situation. Mrs Whitmore was slumped down in the passenger seat, moaning softly. Hell, what had the bastard fed her? Clearly too much of something. She was almost out of it.

There was nothing for it, really, but to take her home, to her husband. A glance at his watch showed eleven thirty-five. Would Nathan Whitmore be home? Luke had read about his hit play, the one he'd written and was directing. What time did plays end? And where was home, anyway? Mrs Whitmore was hardly in a position to tell him and she didn't have any ID on her.

Spying a public telephone box on the next corner Luke decided to try calling him. If his number was in the book, that was. Damn, but this was becoming complicated. Luke almost regretted getting involved in the first place till he took another look at Gemma Whitmore's sweetly innocent face. How could he have left her with that devil?

Luke had a change of luck. Nathan Whitmore's number was in the book and he was home, answering quite quickly.

Luke kept his voice crisp and businesslike, hoping like hell that Nathan Whitmore was a sensible and reasonable man. He'd heard he was a cool customer, but men were not always cool when it came to their wives, especially beautiful young ones like his.

'Mr Whitmore, this is Luke Barton. Sorry to bother you at this hour, but it was an emergency.'

'Do I know you, Mr Barton?' came a rather tired query.

'Not personally. You may have heard of me. I'm an executive at Campbell Jewels. I was recently promoted to sales and marketing manager.'

'Then haven't you rung the wrong person? Any emergency at Campbell Jewels is hardly a concern of mine. Though maybe you could try my father,' he added caustically.

'This has nothing to do with business. It concerns your wife...'

Luke heard the sharp intake of breath on the other end. 'What about my wife?' he demanded with abrupt harshness.

'God, this is awkward.'

'You're beginning to worry me, Mr Barton. Has something happened to Gemma? Is she all right?'

'I think so.'

'You *think* so. God-dammit, man, what do you mean by that?'

'If you'll just let me explain,' Luke complained.

'Explain, then. But be quick!'

'Look, I'll have to start at the beginning. Earlier tonight I dropped into this disco in a pub at North Sydney—looking for my sister, actually—and while I was there I couldn't help noticing Damian Campbell dancing with a woman I soon recognised as your wife.'

Nathan muttered something highly uncomplimentary about his wife's choice of companion.

'I quite agree with you, Mr Whitmore,' Luke said drily, 'which is why I started watching them, and it soon became obvious to me that your wife was under the influence of some kind of narcotic. This place is rather a haunt for drug users, I think. Anyway, when I saw Campbell slip something into her drink without her knowing I realised she wasn't a willing party to what was going on, if you get my drift.'

'I get your drift only too well, Mr Barton,' he said bitterly. 'Can you tell me where exactly this place is? Is my wife still there?'

'No need to worry, Mr Whitmore. When I saw the lie of the land, I took it upon myself to get your wife away from the bastard. I have her with me in my car. She's—er—fallen asleep.'

Luke sensed a wealth of emotion vibrating in the taut silence that followed.

'If you'd give me your address, Mr Whitmore,' Luke offered, 'I'll drive her straight home.'

'Are you sure she's all right? Will she need a doctor?'

'I think all she needs is a good night's sleep, though she's going to have one heck of a hangover in the morning. But yes, Mr Whitmore, I'm pretty sure she's all right.'

Luke committed the address and Nathan Whitmore's directions to memory, grateful that he didn't live at Palm Beach or somewhere as distant as that. Elizabeth Bay wasn't more than a hop, skip and jump from North Sydney.

Nathan Whitmore was pacing up and down the pavement when Luke guided his car into the kerb. He immediately strode over and wrenched open the passenger door. As soon as he unclipped the seatbelt, his unconscious wife slumped sideways out of the car and into her husband's arms. Nathan scooped her up, his face grim.

'I should have killed that bastard the first time he came near her,' he muttered, Luke having no doubt whom he meant.

'She's only asleep, Mr Whitmore,' he reassured. 'I checked her pulse. It's fine.'

'Do you have any idea what he gave her?'

Luke shook his head.

Gemma stirred in his arms. 'Is that you, Nathan?' she said in a tiny, child-like voice.

'Yes, Gemma. It's me.'

She sighed her satisfaction then drifted back into her blessedly unconscious state.

'Help me get her upstairs?' Nathan asked Luke.

Some considerable time later, Luke was perched on the edge of a sofa in an elegantly furnished sitting-room while Nathan Whitmore was supposedly putting his wife to bed.

Nathan had asked Luke to wait so he had. But he was certainly taking his time. He'd been away ages.

Frankly, Luke was beginning to feel concerned over what had happened back in that car park, despite Damian Campbell not having been badly hurt. It was a question of how much he'd seen. Hopefully, he hadn't had time to recognise him, or take down the number-plate of his attacker's vehicle. If he had, Luke could kiss his job at Campbell's goodbye.

'Can I get you a drink, Mr Barton?' Nathan asked on returning to the room. 'I certainly can do with one, but I can make you coffee or tea if you'd prefer.'

'I think a small Scotch wouldn't go amiss,' Luke said.

'I don't think I'll be making mine too small,' his host muttered, and, after handing Luke a conservative amount, poured himself a hefty slug.

There ensued a short, tense conversation where Nathan tried to elicit more details from Luke.

'So you actually hit him.'

'Had to. He's all right, though. I saw him beginning to get to his feet, but I hope to hell he didn't recognise me.'

'He won't be getting to his feet by the time I get through with him,' Nathan said darkly.

Luke frowned. 'Do you think that's a wise idea?'

'No. But the time for caution has passed. The man's a blot on society. He has to be stopped.'

'Stopped?' Luke repeated. 'What do you mean, stopped? Good God, man, you don't mean to... to... ?'

Luke watched, appalled, as Nathan Whitmore's face became a stony mask. Those cool grey eyes of his turned icy cold before they met Luke's over the rim of the glass. 'Don't let your imagination get the better of you, Mr Barton,' he said with a silky smoothness that sent a shiver running down Luke's spine. 'There are many ways to stop a monster other than murder.'

An uneasy silence descended on the room. Luke finished his drink and was standing up to go when a telephone rang somewhere. His host excused himself and left the room, closing the door behind him. Luke could hear his muffled voice but couldn't work out what he was saying. When he finally returned, Luke also couldn't work out the expression on his face. It was most peculiar.

'That was my father,' he explained. 'It seems both our problems have been solved, Mr Barton.'

'Both our problems?'

'With Damian Campbell.'

'Oh? How's that?'

'Our esteemed Mr Campbell has been in a car accident. Wrapped his Ferrari around a telegraph pole a little over an hour ago. Witnesses say he sped out of a hotel car park in North Sydney like a maniac and immediately lost control of the car.' Nathan walked over and poured himself another drink, turning to raise the glass in a mock toast. 'He was killed instantly.'

Luke said nothing as Nathan Whitmore smiled a coldly satisfied smile, then drank.

The first flutterings of consciousness were accompanied by a dull throbbing in Gemma's temples. She moaned softly and pulled the bedclothes up around her neck, squeezing her eyes shut against the pain. The throbbing increased as she surfaced further and another moan fell from her lips.

The mattress dipped beside her and a hand stroked some strands of hair back from her face. 'How are you feeling?' a familiar voice enquired.

'I've got a terrible headache,' she mumbled. Sighing a deep shuddering sigh, she rolled over on to her back where slowly and quite painfully she opened her eyes.

Nathan was sitting on the side of the bed, looking down at her with those beautiful grey eyes of his. Only they didn't look so beautiful at that moment. They looked awful. Dull and sunken, with huge dark rings around them.

Any shock at his appearance was suddenly overridden by Gemma's shock at realising where she was and who she was looking up at. For one mad moment, she wondered if the past fortnight had been some ghastly nightmare and she'd woken to find everything was back as it once had been, and she and Nathan would live happily ever after.

But of course, that wasn't the case. She could tell that just by looking into Nathan's face. Yet what was she doing here? How had she got here? The last thing she remembered was dancing at that disco with Damian and feeling very peculiar.

Her face screwed up with the pain of her throbbing head and the effort to put the pieces together of the night before. Short flashes of memory kept jumping into her head, then skittering away before they came clear. Someone had kissed her, she thought. And held her very tightly. Had that been Nathan? She seemed to recall speaking to Nathan at some stage during the night. Had he shown up at the disco and taken her away from Damian? No, that didn't feel right. There had been some other man...

Gemma's head throbbed ever harder as she tried to remember. God, she must have been blind drunk. Yet she'd only had a couple of glasses of wine earlier in the evening before switching to orange juice. Could someone have spiked her juice with gin, or vodka perhaps?

More flashes of memory started to return, sketchy and quite alarming. She recalled being carried somewhere and then hands undressing her. Her eyes flung wide as that particular memory seemed to be accompanied by an intense wave of sensual pleasure. Dear God, Nathan hadn't, had he?

With a fearful gasp, she lifted the bedclothes to take a quick anxious look at herself, and while she wasn't naked she only had a skimpy bra and bikini pants on. A frantic glance around the room saw her clothes draped over a nearby chair and her jewellery on the bedside table.

'No need to panic,' Nathan said drily. 'I didn't touch you, except in the course of undressing you and putting you to bed. Not that you didn't *want* me to. You were all for it. Fact is, I had the devil of a time getting away from you with my virtue intact. I could have done anything to you I wanted and you would not have objected. It was lucky for me that you eventually passed out again.'

Gemma stared at him. 'I don't believe you!' she ex claimed, horrified by the inner suspicion that what he wa saying was true.

'There's no need to be so appalled at yourself, Gemma It wasn't your fault. Anyone can become wildly uninhib ited and promiscuous while under the influence of certair drugs.'

'*Drugs*!' she gasped, her head reeling.

'That's right. Your dear uncle Damian had been slipping something into your drinks all night.'

She just stared at him.

He shook his head, his eyes reproachful. 'Why did you gc out with him, Gemma? I did warn you his being your uncle wouldn't stop him. Men like him don't have any qualms, or morals, or conscience.'

These last words outraged her so much she was propelled from her frozen horror into a somewhat shaky tirade. 'Isn't that the p...pot calling the kettle black? I've already tolc you a thousand times, Damian has never been anything but a perfect gentleman with me, so why shouldn't I go to a harmless disco with him? Besides, I only have your say-so that he was the one who put drugs in my drinks. Maybe it was someone else,' she argued, already knowing in her heart that she was clutching at straws.

'I don't blame you for not taking my word for anything,' Nathan returned ruefully, 'but I have an independent wit ness who saw everything. A Mr Luke Barton. He's an ex ecutive at Campbell's. He noticed what was happening between you and Campbell and didn't like the look of things. The man's reputation *has* preceded him. When Damian coerced you into the car park outside and started mauling you, he stepped in.'

'S...stepped in? What do you mean?'

'Rescued you, dear heart. Dragged Damian off you, popped him on the chin and took off with you in his car. The fact that you went with him without a whimper might underline my earlier claim that you were not in a fit state to say no to any man. You're damned lucky that Luke is a decent fellow. He could easily have taken over where Damian left off but instead he called me, then brought you home.'

Gemma closed her eyes against the horrors Nathan had just described to her. She didn't want to believe him, for to do so was to accept that everything he had ever said about Damian was true. And everything he had said about *her* was true. She *was* a naïve silly little bitch to have been taken in by someone as deeply evil as Damian obviously was.

The extent of her uncle's wickedness hit her like a punch in the stomach. Good God, the man was vile! But how had he hoped to get away with doing something so...so gross? Drugging her, then...then...

Nausea and an overwhelming feeling of betrayal sent a bitter taste into her mouth and she lashed out at the person closest to her, the one whose own betrayal cut even deeper than Damian's. Her eyes opened in a way they had never opened before, raking over Nathan with a type of coldly cynical gaze which had previously been his sole provence.

'Why didn't you tell this Luke person we were separated?' she asked, her voice hard and bitter. 'Why didn't you have him take me home to Belleview instead of here?'

Nathan seemed startled by her accusatory tone, which infuriated her further. 'You couldn't resist having the opportunity to say, "I told you so", could you? You had to lord it over me, make me feel small and stupid. You had to show me that you had known best all along and that if I'd listened to you this wouldn't have happened.'

Nathan sighed a weary sigh. 'That's not true, Gemma. When Luke rang, all I thought about was your welfare. I had to see for myself that you were all right.'

'You're a liar!' she flung at him wildly, hating the way her heart had turned over at his pretend concern. 'You don't care about me! You've only ever cared about yourself!'

Gemma threw back the bedclothes and climbed out of the bed, snatching up her clothes from the chair and whirling to glare down at a stony-faced Nathan.

'Don't go thinking you're any better than Damian, because you're not! You're both bastards. I hate and despise the pair of you. When I think that I spent this last night in the same bed that you've probably been busy screwing Jody in all week, I want to be sick.'

Nathan stood up, his face ashen. 'Jody hasn't been in this bed. Not once.'

'And I'm supposed to believe that?' she said scoffingly.

His eyes turned sardonic, a wry smile twisting his mouth. 'If you did, I'd probably call you a fool. But it's true, nevertheless.'

'Are you saying you didn't bring her home here the night after the party?'

'No, that's not what I'm saying.'

Her top lip curled with contempt. 'So! You're just playing with words. No doubt she was very happy to accommodate you in all those interesting places and ways your innocent and silly young wife used to shrink from, or be embarrassed over.'

'I never wanted you to do anything you weren't comfortable with, Gemma,' he said stiffly.

She laughed. 'Then why throw me over for an older, more experienced model? Didn't straightforward love-making satisfy you any more? Maybe I should have asked Lenore what she did for you that kept you in her bed for twelve years. Obviously my country-bumpkin technique was a little lacking.'

'That's not true,' Nathan said rather bleakly. 'You know I enjoyed making love to you.'

'How kind of you to say so,' she retorted bitterly. 'I'm so gratified. Of course, there is only so much youth and innocence a man like you can take before he needs a change. Still, all that's water under the bridge now, isn't it? We're over, as you so rightly pointed out to me the last time we met. If I loved you once, I certainly don't any more, so if you're having second thoughts about getting rid of your regular lay then think again. I wouldn't have you back if you crawled on your hands and knees from here to Burke and back. Now, I'm going to have a shower and get dressed, after which I'm going to call Belleview and let them know where I am. I can only hope that they haven't noticed yet that I'm missing.'

'I've already spoken with Byron,' Nathan said, his expression totally unreadable now, his voice low and irritatingly calm. 'He knows where you are.'

'I hope you haven't given him any false hopes,' she warned darkly. 'We both know he wants us to get back together again. But I won't be manipulated. Not any more.'

'I won't deny he seemed pleased to hear you were with me.'

'My God, you really have changed your mind, haven't you? You want me back for some reason. Why, for pity's sake? Has the cost been too high?' she scorned. 'Is Byron's opinion of you so important that you would be prepared to put up with this naïve silly little bitch in your bed every night?'

Nathan flinched at this last remark. 'Please don't keep calling yourself that.'

'Why not? It seems very appropriate, especially after last night, wouldn't you say? I'd have to win the prize for shmuck of the century, wouldn't I? Everyone else knew the sort of person Damian was, even Celeste. But not good old Gemma from Timbuctoo! She thought he was a perfect gentleman—instead he was the worst kind of pervert. I sometimes wonder if there's something about me that attracts that kind of man,' she finished, glaring straight at Nathan.

He visibly blanched and for some unaccountable reason she felt guilty. Lord knew why. He deserved everything she could throw at him, surely!

'Let's not pursue this conversation further,' she suddenly snapped. 'Because there's nothing you could say or do to make me resume our marriage.'

Gemma brushed past Nathan's seemingly frozen body and strode angrily into the bathroom. It felt good to slam the door shut, felt good to snap the taps on, hard and strong. But by the time she had rid herself of her underwear and stepped under the steaming jets of water, tears were running down her face, tears for her lost innocence and her lost love, tears for all the dreams which she had once had and which would never now come true.

There was no evidence of tears, however, by the time she walked into the kitchen to find Nathan sitting up at the breakfast bar, drinking coffee. Gemma was fully composed, if a little fragile. Her headache was only marginally better, and there was a lingering of nausea in her empty stomach.

The clock on the wall said eleven-fifteen.

'I'm going to call a taxi now,' she told him crisply.

He looked up, his eyes betraying nothing as he looked her up and down. 'I think you'd better sit down a while, Gemma. I have something to tell you . . .'

CHAPTER FIVE

GEMMA sat on top of the mullock heap, idly swatting flies and fossicking through the dirt and rocks around her. The likelihood of finding any opal or gemstone of value in Ma's leavings was remote, but Gemma found the mindless activity soothing. She found life back at Lightning Ridge soothing all round.

When she'd stepped off the plane a little over six weeks ago she'd been a quivering wreck.

Twenty-four hours previously she had attended Damian's funeral, staunchly standing by her mother's and grandmother's sides, pretending for their sakes that she still loved her uncle, still held him in high esteem. It had been Byron who had asked this mammoth effort from her, explaining that it would have been totally cruel to blacken the memory of their son and brother. Cruel and unnecessary. What would be gained by exposing what Damian had tried to do the night he died? Byron had argued.

Gemma had already been in too weakened an emotional state to fight her father's wishes. She'd begun to fall apart from the moment Nathan had told her of Damian's fatal car accident. Nathan had tried to be kind in the telling, she supposed, but had clearly been at a loss to understand her tears. Disbelief had eventually changed to a cold anger, when he thought she was grieving for the man.

But it wasn't that at all. She was grieving for the pathetic mess people made of their lives when there was no need. Why couldn't everyone be decent and kind, loving and caring for each other instead of being consumed by their own selfish and self-destructive desires?

Nathan hadn't said a single word to her during the drive back to Belleview later that day. Gemma suspected he'd once thought there had been something more than a platonic relationship between herself and Damian at some stage, and she'd been too emotionally and physically exhausted to try to convince him otherwise. She'd sat in the passenger seat, huddled up and shivering despite it being a reasonably warm spring day.

If it hadn't been for Ava, Gemma believed she might have gone totally over some dark edge that day. But dear sweet Ava had enfolded her against her womanly bosom, fed her and fussed over her then put her to bed with a couple of sleeping pills. By the time Gemma woke late the next morning, the sun had been shining brightly and any serious breakdown had been averted.

Still, by the time the funeral was over a few days later it had been imperative that she get away. Gemma had somehow found just enough courage and spirit left to make that decision, and to follow it through. Both Celeste and Byron had argued with her, saying they wanted to look after her. Even Ava had argued with her, trying reverse psychology in claiming she needed Gemma's company around Belleview.

Gemma had smiled indulgently at this—Ava's days of wishy-washy dependence were well and truly over—then ignored it. She'd ignored all their wishes and booked her flight to Lightning Ridge. All she had promised was that she would write. She'd refused to agree to any return date, simply saying that she would come back when the time was right. She'd apologised to Byron for quitting her job again, but this time, she'd told him, it was for good. If and when she returned to Sydney, she was determined to get her own job, under her own steam.

But would she ever return to Sydney? Gemma wondered, tipping back the brim of the old felt Akruba hat she was wearing and staring around her. There had been a time when she had found nothing pleasing to the eye in the dry, stark landscape around Lightning Ridge. And the lifestyle had bored her to tears

Yet now, she could see a kind of raw beauty in the rocky ridges and the harsh blue sky. And she had welcomed the peace and quiet which came with the territory. The heat was the only thing she was taking some time getting used to again. Gemma pulled a handkerchief from the pocket of her denim cut-offs and wiped a fine layer of sweat from her forehead. She certainly hadn't sweated like this back in Sydney.

'What on earth are you doin' sittin' out here in the sun?' Ma growled at her. 'It's nearly midday, for heaven's sake. Only "mad dogs and Englishmen go out in the midday sun"!'

'Is it really that late?' Gemma replied, scrambling down off the mullock heap and giving Ma a sheepish look. She had developed the habit of daydreaming since returning to the Ridge. Many a time she would just sit, and her mind would start wandering, or simply to blank for ages. The first time she had done it, she'd got a touch of the sun. Not burnt, mind. Gemma's skin wasn't the kind to burn. But she'd developed the most dreadful headache which had lasted for days.

'Just look at you,' Ma went on accusingly. 'You're getting as brown as a berry. Haven't you been usin' your sunscreen?'

'Yes, I have,' Gemma defended. 'Truly. I just have a lot of natural melanin in my skin.'

'A lot of what?'

'Melanin. It's a pigment.'

'It's an excuse, that's what it is. You don't want to be gettin' as many skin cancers as I've got when you're my age, do you? Why don't you make yourself useful,' Ma suggested, 'by gettin' us a good drink while I get the shoppin' out of the truck?'

Ma's idea of a cool drink was always a beer, but Gemma didn't object. She liked a cool beer herself when the temperature got up to thirty-five as it was today. And it was only November! By Christmas they'd be steaming. Ma thought the old dugout was cool compared to the caravan she used to live in. And it probably was, but hardly a patch on the air-conditioning at Belleview. Gemma missed her creature comforts sometimes.

She missed other things too.

Yet it had been good to come back to where she'd been brought up, good for her to get back to basic living. She'd been spoilt down in Sydney. It had made her soft. When troubles had come, she'd started succumbing to self-pity and that was a sorry way to live.

But a few weeks of being around Ma and looking after herself with little or no pampering had done her the world of good. So had not having any television or video to watch. They talked into the night most evenings, and Gemma had at last begun to put her marriage into perspective. Ma had a way of putting things sometimes that made everything seem so clear and simple.

'It was just sex, love,' she'd said about Gemma's feelings for Nathan and his for her. 'Happens all the time. Fact is, most marriages start that way but then kiddies come along and that either makes or breaks things. Bein' a parent makes one grow up, you see. Doesn't always happen like that, of course, specially with the men. Some men never grow up, love. That's the truth of it and there's no use breakin' your heart over that kind.'

Gemma didn't really think Nathan was that kind. He was a far more complex individual with deep dark hang-ups from a past that someone as simple as Ma would never guess at. But it was still good to hear her homespun philosophies which indeed gave Gemma plenty to think about.

'You don't think I ever really loved Nathan either, do you?' she'd remarked late one night.

'Nah. He bowled you over with his good looks and his know-how, that's all. How could you really love him? You didn't even get to know him. Except in the biblical sense,' Ma had cackled, leaning over to dig Gemma in the ribs.

Although Gemma had laughed too at the time, she was still a long way from getting over Nathan. And she was long way from forgetting what it was like when he made love to her. Many a night she would lie in the narrow, uncomfortable single bed she'd slept in as a child, her body encased in a simple cotton nightshirt, and think of her experiences as the wife of a man who had done to her what he had once vowed to do. He had made her body attuned to his, had made her respond even when she hadn't wanted to, had made her want him with a want that had nothing to do with love and everything to do with lust. In that respect, Ma was probably right.

Sometimes her skin would actually crawl with desire, and she would toss and turn, aching to have him there in bed with her to drive the madness away. She wanted to cling to him, move with him, dig her nails into him. She wanted ... oh, she just wanted. There was no rhyme or reason to her frustrations, she knew that. She'd become a mindless victim to a devilishly sexy man who had taken her blank virgin body and programmed it with responses that only he could trigger, and needs that only he could soothe.

Which was why it would be a long time before she would forget him. Maybe she never would if what she suspected turned out to be true.

But that didn't mean she had to fall apart over him. Hell, no. She was made of tougher stuff than that, she hoped.

Gemma walked into the relative cool of the dugout and was bending down to extract a couple of cans of beer from the small gas fridge in the corner when the dizziness struck. Instinctively, she sank down to the ground and put her head between her knees, which was how Ma found her when she walked in.

'Good God!' Ma threw the shopping bags on the kitchen table and raced over to squat down beside Gemma. 'What is it? What's wrong?'

Gemma slowly raised her head. The black dots had gone from in front of her eyes but she still felt cold and clammy. 'I ... I nearly fainted.'

'See what happens when you don't do as you're told? You've probably got sunstroke again.'

'I don't think it's sunstroke,' she said quietly, slumping down on the floor. 'I think I'm pregnant.'

Ma's eyebrows shot up. 'Good lord! Have you been to see the doc?'

'No.'

'Then how can you be sure?'

'I haven't had a period in ages, my breasts are sore and I've been feeling like throwing up the last few mornings.'

'And you didn't tell me?'

'I . . . I was trying to pretend it wasn't true.'

Ma sat down on the floor beside her with a thud, a troubled frown making more wrinkles on her already deeply wrinkled face. 'Don't you want this baby, love?'

Gemma sighed. 'In any other circumstances, I would be over the moon, but it's hardly the right time, is it? I always vowed that no child of mine would have the disadvantages I had, being brought up by a single parent with no brothers or sisters.'

'You're not plannin' on doin' away with it, are you?'

'Good lord, no!'

'Didn't think so.' Ma gnawed on her bottom lip for a while then looked over at Gemma. 'I'll help you any way I can but this is hardly the ideal place to bring up a baby. You better than anyone should know that.'

Gemma glanced around her at the primitive surroundings. 'Yes, I know.'

'What do you think you might do?'

'I haven't thought that far ahead yet.'

'How far are you gone, do you know?'

'A little over two months,' she said, deliberately adding a week to the truth. She'd told Ma just about everything that had happened between herself and Nathan since her last visit to Lightning Ridge, except the rape. She had substituted a fierce argument for that incident.

Ma gave her a sharp look. 'It *is* your husband's, isn't it?'

Gemma's dismay was acute. 'Oh, Ma . . . not you too. Of course it's Nathan's. I've never been to bed with any other man. I know you don't believe I loved Nathan any more than he loved me but you're wrong. I did. I would never be unfaithful to him.'

Ma reached out to curve a comforting hand over Gemma's shoulder. 'I believe you, love. But I had to ask. Come on, let's get you up off this floor and have that cool drink. Unless you think you should lie down.'

'I'm all right now. Really. I'll just sit at the table with you.'

'I'll get you a lemonade. No more beer for you, young woman. Ladies havin' babies don't drink beer.'

Gemma didn't think a can or two of light beer would do any harm but she wasn't going to argue.

'Do you still love him?' Ma asked as she handed Gemma a can of lemonade and sat down with her beer.

Gemma's stomach contracted. Did she? To be honest, she wasn't sure. Her shrug was full of confusion. 'Maybe. Probably. I don't really know. I still think about him a lot. He's a hard man to forget.'

'I'll have to meet this devil one day, see just what it is that gets the women in so badly.'

Gemma sighed. 'I doubt you'll ever get to meet him. He's not likely to drop in out here for morning tea, is he?'

'Oh, I don't know, love. Once you tell him about the baby, I wouldn't mind bettin' he hotfoots it out here like a shot out of a gun.'

'I'm not going to tell him about the baby.'

Ma almost had apoplexy. 'Not tell him about the baby? Good God, whyever not, you stupid girl?'

Gemma bristled. 'He doesn't want me any more and he certainly won't want this baby,' she said firmly.

'Rubbish! He married that other woman cause she was havin' his baby, and he never fancied her nearly as much as he obviously fancied you. As for his not wantin' you any more, I can't believe you believe that nonsense. The man was crazy about you at one stage, so crazy that he married you after sayin' he would never marry again! OK, so he went off his head with jealousy when he thought you were having an affair and did some crazy things. But a lot of men do crazy things when they're insanely jealous. I'll bet he's already sorry he chucked you out.'

Gemma recalled that brief moment the morning after Damian's death, when she'd accused Nathan of wanting her back again. He certainly hadn't responded to that, nor had he done anything later to persuade her to resume their marriage. Yet he'd had plenty of opportunity, especially with her in such an emotionally vulnerable state.

'I don't deny Nathan was jealous,' she said with a sigh. 'But he doesn't love me, and it's perfectly clear he doesn't want me back. If he did, he'd have called, or written, or come up here personally. No, I won't use this baby to get back a man who doesn't love me.'

'Then you're a silly little fool. What if he finds out anyway then tries to take the baby away from you?'

Gemma stared at Ma, wide-eyed.

'He's a rich man, isn't he? You said he inherited a fortune from his grandparents on top of all the money those plays of his bring in.'

Gemma nodded.

'Amazing what money can buy,' was Ma's dry comment.

'Nathan wouldn't do that!' Gemma gasped.

'How do you know? You yourself said you didn't really know him. What if he's always wanted a son and you have a boy? What if he becomes as mad for the child as he once was for you? The man has *legal* rights as well. He might not need to bribe anyone to get custody of his child. All he needs is a sympathetic judge.'

Gemma was shaking her head. 'Nathan would never do something like that.'

'For pity's sake, don't start puttin' your head in the sand, love. You might be sorry one day if you do. It's time to be a realist, not a fluffy-headed romantic. You have to think of your own welfare as well. Bringin' a baby up all alone is one hell of a job in this day and age. It takes a lot of time and money for one thing.'

'I have time and money,' Gemma countered irritably, sorry now that she had told Ma. 'If I want more money, I can get myself a smart solicitor, divorce Nathan and take him to the cleaners.'

'Oh, lovely. Is that what city life has done to you? Turned you into a money-grubbin', hard-hearted little bitch?'

Shock at Ma's harsh words sent Gemma's eyes rounding.

'Don't look at me like that,' Ma scorned with a flick of her hand. 'You're no babe-in-the-woods any more. You're a married woman and you're going to have your husband's child. This is no time for a divorce!'

'You don't understand,' Gemma wailed. 'Nathan won't want this child!'

'Why won't he want it? I bet he'd be tickled pink.'

Gemma was about to blurt out the truth when something kept her mouth shut. Instead, she dropped her eyes and shook her head. 'He probably won't believe the baby's his,' she muttered.

'Rubbish! There's tests for that sort of thing these days. You could prove it.'

'Ma, stop it,' Gemma groaned. 'Please. I…I don't want to tell Nathan about the baby.'

'You're being a stubborn fool!'

'Maybe. But it's my life and my baby.'

'That's a very naïve thing to say, Gemma.'

'I am not naïve!' she cried.

'Then put your actions where your mouth is and tell him about the baby. Make him put his uninterest along with his intention to divorce you both in writin'.'

Gemma threw up her hands in defeat. 'All right!' she bit out, the 'naïve' accusation still stinging. 'I'll go to Sydney and tell him.'

'No, you won't. We'll ring him and get him to come out here. I want to see this devil for meself. And I want to see how he takes your news about the baby.'

'How on earth are we going to get him to come all this way without telling him about the baby first?'

'I'll think of something, love. Never you fear.'

CHAPTER SIX

HE WAS coming.

Gemma still could not believe it. Ma had gone back into town the previous afternoon and brought back a pregnancy testing kit from the chemist. When it had returned a resoundingly positive result, she'd driven back into town and rung Nathan at home, getting on to him immediately.

Apparently, he was flying up this morning, then hiring a car, refusing Ma's offer to pick him up at the airport. Gemma estimated that if the plane was on time he should arrive around eleven. Since it was just before ten, she still had over an hour to wait, yet already she was highly agitated.

'I want to know what you told Nathan to make him come,' she asked Ma again as he paced up and down. 'You told him about the baby, didn't you?'

'Nope.'

'Why won't you tell me what you said?'

'Because.'

Gemma stamped her foot in frustration. 'That's no answer!'

'It's the only one you're going to get,' Ma retorted firmly. 'Now go make yourself pretty for your husband. And put on some fresh clothes.'

'I will not! I look perfectly all right in these shorts and top which were put on fresh this morning. It's what I always wear and I'm not changing it for anyone, least of all *him*.'

Ma shrugged and had to battle to stop a smile from pulling at her lips. Little did Gemma know that in her present rigout she would hold more attractions for a jaded city man than the most dolled-up glamour-puss.

There was so much for him to feast his eyes upon.

Gemma's long shapely legs would have made a dancer proud, and every inch of their firm tanned expanse was on display, her short shorts only barely covering her buttocks. If she bent over, they didn't even do that. Then there was her singlet top which might have been reasonably modest on a less well-endowed girl. But Gemma's pregnancy had made her already full bust more than memorable, her darkening and distended nipples clearly outlined against the thin white material.

'I'm not putting any make-up on either,' Gemma pouted. 'Neither am I going to do anything fancy with my hair!'

Now Gemma's face had never really needed make-up, with her clear olive skin and thickly lashed brown eyes, her high cheekbones that flushed prettily when her blood was up, and her generous lips, which did likewise. As for her hair...at the moment it was falling around her face with that slightly dishevelled and tousled look which could sometimes be sexier than all the sleek coiffures in the world.

Ma had no doubt that when Nathan Whitmore arrived he would not be able to take his eyes off his lovely young wife, nor would he be able to stop himself from wanting her back in his bed, as he had obviously wanted her from the first moment he'd set eyes upon her.

'The least you can do is put some lipstick on,' Ma complained.

'What for? I don't think you've been listening to me these past few weeks, Ma. Nathan doesn't want me any more. And I certainly don't want him. God help you if you've been telling him I do. You...you haven't, have you?' she asked in a panic.

'Certainly not! Look, if you must know, all I told him was that you hadn't been very well.'

Gemma's expression was sceptical. 'Oh, come now, Ma, that wouldn't have got Nathan charging up here. He'd have simply told you to take me to a doctor.'

'Er—we don't have that kind of doctor up here.'

'What kind of doctor? Are you talking about a gynaecologist?'

'No, a psychiatrist.'

Gemma's mouth fell open then snapped shut. 'You told him I was mad as a hatter?'

'Something like that.'

'Ma, how could you?'

Ma shrugged, the action making her huge body jiggle like jelly. 'It was real easy.'

Gemma groaned. 'Nathan's the one who's going to be mad as a hatter when he finds out you lied to him.'

'Couldn't you pretend to be a bit loony?' Ma asked hopefully.

Gemma pulled a face at her. 'Very funny.'

'Look, it got him up here, didn't it? I'll straighten things out as soon as he arrives, then when you tell him the real reason you wanted to see him he'll soon forget my little white lie.'

'You've never said a truer word, Ma,' was Gemma's dry remark, her stomach turning over as she tried to imagine what Nathan's reaction to her pregnancy would be. 'God, this is going to be a disaster!' she grimaced.

'No, it isn't. It'll settle a lot of things in your mind, and it'll give the two of you a chance to come to some agreement where the baby is concerned. As I said before, Gemma, the man has rights. Best you see what part he wants to play in the child's life right from the start. Maybe he'll only want to give you financial support, but I have a feelin' in me water that he'll want more than that. Now, I'm going to make us a nice cup of tea then we'll talk about somethin' else for the next hour, OK?'

Gemma sighed her defeat. 'OK.'

Ma turned away to walk over to the primitive kitchenette, filling the kettle from the old tap which connected to the tank outside and lighting the small gas primus stove. She wasn't sure how things would turn out today with Nathan and Gemma, but she was one of the old school who believed marriage was a very serious business. It was not to be entered into lightly.

It was not to be thrown away lightly, either. Gemma had married this man and she was having his baby. They both had a responsibility to try again, especially since it seemed that what had broken them up had been a series of unfortunate mishaps, plus a healthy dose of male jealousy.

OK, so they didn't seem to have much going for them at the moment except sex, but that was not to be scoffed at, in Ma's opinion. Many a couple deeply in love had broken up because of problems in the bedroom. With a bit of luck, this baby might make Mr Nathan Whitmore see his wife as more than a sex object. Maybe he would begin to appreciate her generous and genuinely loving soul, and maybe, with a bit of luck, some of that capacity for love might rub off on to his own obviously lacking and selfish male heart.

Whatever, Ma believed she had done the right thing in organising this meeting. No matter what happened, Gemma had to tell the man about his baby. After that, it was up to them.

Gemma was in a state by the time eleven came and went without Nathan showing up. Her feelings swung between disappointment and relief. She kept walking outside and staring down the dusty track, squinting her eyes against the glare of the sun. A couple of times a cloud of dust in the distance sent her heart racing and a squirming feeling into her stomach, but no car materialised their way. The third time it happened, the butterflies stayed away. But then a car suddenly came into view, and everything inside Gemma flipped over. She raced back inside, pale and shaking.

'He's coming,' she whispered.

Ma stood up, a formidable figure despite being dressed in an old blue floral dress that should have been consigned to a charity clothes bin years ago. She put a steadying hand on Gemma's shoulders and looked her straight in the eye. 'Calm yourself, love. He's just a man.'

Gemma swallowed, knowing Ma was saying it as she saw it, but she didn't have all the facts. Gemma was worried sick over how Nathan was going to react to the news that a baby had been conceived that awful afternoon. It was ironic that she had first accepted such a possibility with such optimism, thinking a pregnancy could be used as a weapon to get Nathan back. She knew better now. Only Ma's argument that Nathan could cause her problems later if she didn't tell him about the baby up front had made her agree to this course of action. Still, that didn't mean she had to look forward to relaying the news.

'Don't skulk away in here,' Ma reprimanded. 'Come outside and meet him with your head held high and some starch in your backbone. Don't let him think you're afraid of him.'

'I'm not afraid of him,' she said stiffly. She was afraid of herself. She'd always been afraid of herself where Nathan was concerned.

Gemma walked out into the sunlight with Ma just as a blue Corolla pulled up where the track ended, twenty or so metres away. She lifted a hand to shade her eyes from the sunlight, but it was shaking so much she put it down again.

Nathan climbed out from behind the wheel of the dusty car, looking as though he'd just stepped out of an air-conditioned city office. He was dressed in a pale grey business suit, a crisp white shirt and dark grey tie. Ma, who had never seen Nathan before, sucked in a startled breath as he started walking towards them, the sun dancing on his blond hair as the elegantly lazy stride of his long legs covered the ground with surprising speed.

'Hell, girl,' she muttered under her breath. 'You didn't tell me he was *that* good-looking.'

'He's just a man, Ma,' Gemma countered with perverse humour, but her heart was pounding in her chest at the sight of her handsome husband, in much the same way as it had always done.

His beautiful grey eyes flicked from Ma to Gemma as he approached, disconcerting her when they travelled slowly down her body then up again. God, but she despised herself for the way her pulse-rate was going haywire. But at least she wasn't fool enough to mistake her reactions for love any more. She knew good old lust when she felt it these days. And much as she didn't want still to lust after Nathan, it was clear that she did.

'You look surprisingly well,' he said curtly, 'for some-one's who's having a nervous breakdown.'

'Before any more is said,' Ma intervened swiftly, 'Gemma is perfectly well, as you've so rightly noticed. I lied to get you out here, Mr Whitmore. I'm not sorry I did, either.'

Nathan's glare was withering as his eyes shifted to Ma but she didn't flinch an inch.

'I hope you have a very good reason,' he grated out. 'If Gemma's face is anything to go by, she doesn't seem to agree with you, Mrs—er...'

'Call me Ma. The truth is, Mr Whitmore, that Gemma has something important to tell you and I wanted to be with her when she did.'

'Why?' he returned with a slicing edge to his voice. 'What did you think I would do to her? What has she been telling you about me?'

'Nothing I haven't seen for myself these few short mo-ments, Mr Whitmore,' Ma returned, blood-pressure mak-ing her face go all red. 'My, but you're a cold bastard, aren't you? My Gemma will be well out of being married to you!'

'I dare say there are others who agree with you, madam,' he said drily. 'As for my being cold...' He peeled off his suit jacket and loosened his tie, undoing the top button on his shirt. 'I feel far from cold at the moment. But surely you haven't dragged me all the way out here just to ask for a di-vorce, Gemma. A telephone call to Zachary would have sufficed.'

'This isn't about our divorce, Nathan,' she snapped, an-noyed with herself for having stared so when he started to undress. 'I will leave the legalities of that up to you, since you were the one who was so anxious to get rid of me. An-other little problem had cropped up that Ma felt you should know about.'

Nathan arched his left eyebrow, a steely glance slanting Ma's way.

She drew herself up as tall as her five feet and very ro-tund figure allowed. 'I think we should go inside,' she said quite haughtily.

'Amen to that,' Nathan drawled, ducking as he went ahead through the low, roughly framed door.

'Arrogant bastard,' Ma hissed at Gemma. 'But sexy as all hell. I can see why you're having trouble forgetting him.'

Gemma smothered a silent groan. God, the moment he'd climbed out of that car and looked her over with that lazily sensual gaze of his her wits had been in danger of becoming scrambled. As for her body... that didn't bear thinking about. It wasn't fair that any man should have that kind of power, but even Ma was feeling it. What chance did *she* have when she'd already spent so much time in his bed, when he'd successfully taught her to respond to as little as a glance, or a seemingly innocent touch?

Nathan stood behind one of the chairs at the large wooden table that dominated the single-room dugout, not bothering to hide his feelings as he glanced around. One could almost see his lips curl with distaste at such primitive living conditions.

'Do sit down, Nathan,' Gemma said sharply. 'The chairs might be pretty rough but they're solid. Would you like a cool drink?'

'No, thank you. I'd like you to get on with telling me why I'm here,' he said, not a ruffle in his cool demeanour as he pulled out a chair and sat down.

Gemma swallowed, then plunged in before she could think better of it. 'I won't beat around the bush,' she said swiftly. 'The fact is, Nathan, I'm pregnant. And before you say another word, let me assure you that it is yours. If you don't believe me I'm quite prepared to have the appropriate tests once the child is born.'

Was she imagining it or did all the blood drain from his face?

She must have imagined it because the next thing she knew he was laughing. Both Ma and Gemma stared at him with their mouths open.

'If ever I was to believe in a just God,' Nathan said after one last harsh bark of laughter, 'then this would be the moment.'

Gemma had no idea what he was talking about. All she knew was that she found his laughter a hurtful and hateful thing. Finally, his eyes dropped from hers, his shoulders sagging a little. Gemma despised herself for feeling an unaccountable pity for him. But when he looked up again, any pity died in the face of his implacable expression.

'Don't you mean *unjust*?' she snapped. 'You don't think I *want* this baby, do you?'

Their eyes locked, hers projecting all the anger and bitterness that had festered in her heart over his treatment of her.

'I wish to speak to my wife alone,' he ground out, throwing Ma an uncompromising glance.

Ma looked uncertainly at Gemma, who nodded, not trusting herself to speak at that moment. She was too flustered.

Sighing, Ma stood up. 'I won't be far away,' she warned Nathan as she reluctantly left the dugout.

Gemma glared at Nathan across the table, finding solace in the righteous fury bubbling up inside her. It was better than looking at him and thinking how damned attractive he was or what she might do if he had the gall to suggest their getting back together again. God, but she had to be sick even to consider such a thing. The man had never loved her. He had used her and abused her. She had to fight this weakness within her, had to fight it to the death!

'Well?' she snapped. 'What is it you have to say to me that couldn't be said in front of Ma?'

His eyes darkened to slate as they raked over her angry face, seemingly assessing how she felt about the situation. Even so, she wasn't ready for what he was about to say. Yet she should have been, shouldn't she? She should have known, all along, what he would consider the ideal solution to her having conceived that awful afternoon.

'I presume you want an abortion,' he said tautly. 'And I presume you expect me to pay for it. In the circumstances, I can appreciate your—'

'No,' she cut in coldly. 'I won't want an abortion. I am going to have this baby, come hell or high water.'

His pained bewilderment seemed very real. 'But *why*, for pity's sake? Every time you look at the child you will remember how it was conceived. You'll end up hating it as you obviously hate me.'

Her look changed quickly from shock to scorn. 'How little you know about me, Nathan. But I don't have to explain my motivations to you. Or my feelings. I have informed you of the baby's existence, and my intention to have it. I would like to know what your intentions are. Do you wish merely to be its father in name only? Or do you wish to play some role in its upbringing? Either way, I can assure you that you *are* going to pay, and pay dearly.'

Nathan glared at her. 'So that's the bottom line, is it? Money. You're going to have the baby because it will squeeze a bigger divorce settlement out of me.'

Gemma was almost numb with outrage. But be damned if she was going to let him have the last word. 'And why not?' she taunted. 'If that's what I want. This silly little naïve bitch has finally grown up, Nathan. I'm going to screw you like you screwed me. Without mercy. And totally without love.'

Now the blood really did drain from his face, and for a horrible moment Gemma was filled with remorse. What had possessed her to say such wicked words? Was it because of the desire that kept pricking at her flesh? Did she hope to wipe away all her feelings for this man by wallowing in hate and revenge?

'So how much money *do* you want, Gemma?' he ground out at long last. 'Spit it out.'

'You think all I want is money?' she flung at him.

'Then what *is* it that you want?' he said, a weary exasperation in his voice. 'Tell me, and if it's possible I'll give it to you.'

She gave a small, hysterical little laugh. Tears pricked at her eyes and she looked down at the table. 'What if I told you that I want you back, as my husband and the father of my baby? What if I told you I want your love? Can you give me that, Nathan?'

He didn't say a word.

'Just as I thought,' she said bitterly, blinking back the tears. When she looked up again, her eyes were bright and hard. 'In that case, I'll settle for you being a real father to this baby, not just a cheque-book one.'

'I've never shrunk from my responsibilities as a father.'

'How noble of you.'

'I think we've already established that I'm not noble, Gemma. But I do have my own peculiar brand of honour. If you're prepared to overlook my obvious shortcomings as a husband, I'm prepared to have another go at our marriage. What do you say?'

Gemma shot to her feet, instant indignation firing up her blood. 'I say to hell with you, Nathan Whitmore! I don't want some sacrificial lamb as a husband. Neither do I want a husband who doesn't love me. Who in hell do you think you are, making me an offer like that? Take your guilt and shove it, buster! Go back to Sydney and your precious Jody. I'm sure you won't have to feel guilty about screwing the likes of her! And if she gets pregnant I'm sure she'll rush off and have an abortion before you can say Jack Robinson!'

'What's going on in here?' Ma raced in, all bothered and breathless. 'What's all the shouting about?'

Gemma was almost beside herself. '*He's* what the shouting's all about,' she cried, pointing at an ashen-faced Nathan with a shaking hand. 'First, he wanted me to have an abortion and then when I said no to that he magnanimously suggested I come back to Sydney with him and play happy families!'

'Well, what's wrong with that?' Ma said, clearly flummoxed by Gemma's attitude. 'Sounds like common sense to me. Surely you're not thinkin' of havin' a baby all by yourself out here and bringin' it up alone, are you, when you have a perfectly good husband who wants to take care of you both?'

Gemma could not believe what she was hearing. Ma, whom she trusted and relied upon, turning against her! 'But I won't be alone,' she argued fiercely. 'I'll have *you*!'

'For how long, love? I'm old and getting older every day. I'd love to have you and the baby here, but it's not practical. Just look at this place. It's a dump. Surely you want more for your son or daughter than this.' She came forward and took Gemma's trembling hands in her large gnarled ones. 'Give it a go, love. If it doesn't work out then at least you won't reproach yourself for never trying.'

'How can it work out when we don't love each other?' Gemma groaned.

'But you will both love the child,' Ma insisted, 'and out of that love you might learn to love each other.'

'Who says we will both love the child?' Gemma muttered, knowing in her heart that Nathan, for one, wouldn't. *He* was the one who didn't want a constant reminder of what he had done, not her.

'If you come with me, Gemma,' Nathan said in a low, intense voice, 'I promise I will do my best to make reparation for what I have done. You won't believe me, I know, but I never meant to hurt you.'

'But you did.'

'Yes...yes, I did,' he confessed. 'I have had plenty of time lately to think about what I've done and regret it deeply. If you're generous enough to give me a second chance, I won't let you down again. And I won't let our child down, either. And who knows? Maybe Ma is right. Maybe we can learn to love each other properly this time. I, for one, would like to think it was possible...'

Gemma stared at him. God, but he was clever. Who would have thought that a few minutes ago he had coldly been discussing an abortion? What lay behind his offer? she puzzled cynically. Did he want her back in his bed? Or was it once again a matter of getting back into Byron's good books?

Gemma didn't understand how much his father's good opinion mattered to him, and Byron would be less than impressed when he learnt she was having Nathan's baby, but Nathan was still divorcing her.

'Now, Gemma,' Ma said by her side. 'The man can't do more than that, can he? Go with him, love. Give him a second chance.'

Gemma had no intention of blithely going back to Nathan, baby or no baby. She had not forgotten, nor forgiven what he had done to her. He could think again if he thought his probably insincere and highly manipulative apology just now would set the record straight.

'I will come back to Sydney with you,' she told him. 'But I won't be living with you. I want a house of my own. And a decent allowance.'

'Now, Gemma,' Ma started. 'Don't be so stubborn. You—'

'No, Ma,' Gemma cut in firmly. 'I won't be swayed on this. I've made up my mind.'

'You can have the house up at Avoca if you like,' Nathan offered in such a silky-smooth voice that Gemma was immediately suspicious. 'And ten thousand a month. Is that enough?'

'That's more than generous, love,' Ma said.

'It certainly is,' Gemma bit out, her eyes locking with her husband's. His returning gaze was disconcertingly bland. Gemma knew that Nathan had a habit of wiping his face of all emotion when his mind was at its most active. It wasn't like him to fall meekly in with her demands like that. What devious plan was he hatching to get her to come back to him? Did he hope to use sex again to bend her to his will?

She almost laughed at this thought. For he didn't need a devious plan, did he? He'd put in the ground work long ago. All he had to do was press the right buttons again and she would probably be his for the taking.

Gemma decided it was fortunate he didn't seem to realise that. Or did he?

Damn, but she was a fool to put herself anywhere near the man, especially now when she was still obviously suffering withdrawal symptoms from being in his bed. Maybe if she waited a few months, till her body was large and clumsy with her pregnancy, there would be no danger of his being able—or even *wanting*—to seduce her.

Nathan glanced at his watch. 'I hate to hurry you but if we're to catch this afternoon's flight you should change and pack.'

'I see no reason for any hurry,' Gemma countered. 'Frankly, I would like to spend Christmas up here with Ma. I'll fly down some time in the new year.'

Nathan's face darkened at this. Even Ma frowned.

'I don't like you staying here in this heat and under these conditions,' he argued.

'She's been feeling the heat,' Ma put in, which brought an exasperated glare from Gemma.

'Well, you *have*,' Ma insisted. 'And she's been having a bit of morning sickness. Hasn't been to see a doctor yet either, though the test from the chemist said she was pregnant enough for two babies. I think your husband's right, Gemma. The sooner you get back to Sydney, the better. I'll pack for you if you like.'

Gemma knew when she was beaten. 'No,' she sighed. 'I'll do it myself. Are you sure there'll be a spare seat on the plane for me?' she asked Nathan, despite already knowing that it was rare for the flights to be full at this time of the year.

'I've already booked you one.'

This presumption irritated her. 'Why on earth would you do that? You didn't know I was pregnant when you arrived.'

'I thought I might have to take you back to Sydney with me to see a shrink, remember?'

'Oh...yes...I forgot about that.'

'I'll take Mr Whitmore for a walk while you change, love,' Ma generously offered. 'Maybe he'd like to see an old-fashioned opal mine in the raw.'

Gemma watched wryly as Ma took Nathan's arm and escorted him outside. She was chatting happily away to him before they even hit the sunshine.

Another female conquest, Gemma thought bitterly. And so easily done too. Handsome men had it too easy, especially when they were rich as well.

But Nathan wasn't going to have it easy this time, Gemma decided with a further hardening of her heart. It would take a lot for him to ever win her trust or her love again. Frankly, it would take a darned miracle!

CHAPTER SEVEN

'CAN we talk, Gemma?'

The plane had just taken off from Lightning Ridge, and Gemma was in the process of uncurling her nervous grip from the armrests when Nathan spoke. She slanted cool eyes his way.

'Talk, Nathan? That's a new one for you, isn't it?'

'Drop the sarcasm, Gemma. It doesn't become you.'

'I don't give a fig if it becomes me or not. I'm not going to pretend to be happy about this situation. I didn't appreciate being coerced into coming back to Sydney today. And I don't appreciate your arrogantly assuming that I will do what you wish. My days of doing what you wish are well and truly over, Nathan.'

'I realise that. But there are more people's wishes to consider than mine. The child you're carrying will be Kirsty's brother or sister, something she's always wanted. Could we try to come to a more amicable arrangement for *her* sake, perhaps?'

Kirsty...

Gemma hadn't thought of Kirsty.

Her heart turned over. The poor love had had a rough deal the past few years, what with her parents divorcing and then her father marrying a girl only a few years older than herself, someone Kirsty had looked upon more as *her* friend than her father's. Kirsty had only just recently come to terms with Gemma's marriage to her father. To announce she was expecting Nathan's baby in the same breath as she was divorcing him would distress the teenager terribly.

'Poor Kirsty,' Gemma murmured.

'We could at least put off the divorce for a while,' Nathan suggested. 'She doesn't know about our separation. Since she began boarding at St Brigit's, she's been so much happier, and Lenore didn't want to say or do anything to upset her again.'

Gemma knew he was referring to the incident where Kirsty had walked in on her mother kissing Zachary Marsden. Gemma herself had been shocked when first told of the affair till she was informed that Zachary was in the process of divorcing his wife, who had been the first to say that their marriage should end. She had also fallen in love with someone else. They had been waiting till their younger son finished his high-school exams at the end of the year before dropping the bombshell that his parents no longer loved each other.

Gemma could understand how such things happened but she still found divorce a terribly sad thing, especially where children were concerned. It turned her mind to her own child, doomed before it was even born to eventually having divorced parents. Unless that miracle happened...

She turned to look at Nathan's coolly composed face and knew that miracle would never happen. He would never love her as she wanted to be loved because he didn't have it in him to love a woman like that. Lenore had once told her not to throw Nathan away, because to do so would be to destroy him.

Lenore was wrong. He'd already been destroyed years before Lenore had even met him. His mother had been the destroyer. His mother and that other evil old bitch he'd lived with when he'd been little more than a boy.

Gemma felt so sure of this that she would have sworn to it on a stack of bibles. And while this appreciation of the forces that had shaped Nathan's personality brought a message of understanding for the man sitting beside her, it did not change the facts. Gemma could not risk putting herself in his hands again, for where women were concerned they were warped hands.

But neither could she deliberately destroy other people. Kirsty could not cope with another divorce just now.

'I don't want to be the cause of making Kirsty miserable,' she said with a ragged sigh. 'I'm prepared to delay our divorce indefinitely, if that will help. I can't see myself ever wanting to marry again, anyway.'

'I've made you bitter,' he said, so bleakly that Gemma was startled.

'Bitter?' she repeated. 'I wouldn't say bitter. I've simply become a realist instead of a romantic. You should be pleased, Nathan. I now look at the world in much the same light you do.'

'And you think that would please me?' he said grimly.

'Well, it certainly didn't please you when I was an innocent little thing with rose-coloured glasses.'

'You pleased me well enough,' he grated out, a muscle twitching in his jaw.

'For a while, maybe.'

'Can we talk of other things?' he snapped.

'Like what?'

'Did you know that your parents married two weeks ago?'

'Yes, of course. They wrote to me about it.'

'Yet you didn't come back to attend,' he said, almost accusingly, she thought.

'No. They understood why I didn't. I sent them a card and a gift with my best wishes. Don't tell me *you* went?'

'Byron wanted me to be his best man, so I could hardly refuse.'

'Despite despising the woman he was marrying?' Gemma said archly.

'Celeste's not as bad as I thought she was,' came the grudging admission.

'Good God, I don't believe it,' Gemma mocked. 'Next thing you'll be telling me you believe I didn't have an affair with Damian.'

'I know you didn't.'

Gemma gasped her shock.

'If you had,' Nathan went on, 'you would not have taken the stance you took today. I recognise righteous indignation when I see it, Gemma. And I recognise an embittered heart. You wouldn't hate me as much as you obviously do unless you were totally innocent of any wrongdoing. I'm only sorry that my view of the world and the people in it was so jaundiced that I couldn't trust what was obvious to everyone else.'

'What is this, Nathan? All this apologising is making me nervous. I keep wondering what you want.'

He darted her a wry look. 'You really have grown up a lot, haven't you?'

'It happens. So out with it? What *do* you want?'

He shrugged. 'No more than what I said in front of Ma. I want you to give our marriage—and me—a second chance.'

'Why should I? I don't love you any more.'

'A marriage can survive without romantic love. I didn't love Lenore, and we were reasonably happy for twelve years. We also gave Kirsty a secure and stable home life, something a child has a right to, don't you think?'

'Might I remind you that your marriage to Lenore eventually ended in divorce right at a time in Kirsty's life when she was at her most vulnerable—her teenage years? Might I also remind you that Lenore obviously pleased you a lot more in bed than I did? No, Nathan, I will not put myself back in a position where I will worry over my performance all the time, and where I will wonder whose bed you are in behind my back. I could perhaps bear your not loving me, but I could not bear your being unfaithful. Which reminds me, how's Jody these days?'

'I am not having an affair with Jody,' Nathan bit out. 'My only relationship with her nowadays is strictly professional.'

'No kidding. What are you doing for sex, then? I can't believe you're doing without. Not you, Nathan.'

His scowl carried frustration. 'Would you believe anything I said? I doubt it. Yes, you're quite right,' he swept on savagely. 'I've been bonking everything in sight. Does that make you happy?'

'Yes.' Her voice was very hard, and very, very bitter. 'And I want you to *keep* bonking everything in sight, because if you ever come near me again, God help me, Nathan, I might do you damage.'

'Maybe the day will come when you *want* me to come near you,' he snarled.

She laughed. 'I can't see that day coming too quickly.'

'I wouldn't be too sure of that.'

Her eyes snapped round to glare at him. 'I'm warning you, Nathan.'

His eyes narrowed as he glared right back at her. 'No, I'm warning you, Gemma. Don't push me too far. I'm doing my best here to do the right thing by you and this baby. But that doesn't mean I'll be your whipping boy. OK, so you won't have me back in your bed. I can understand that. But that doesn't mean I have to like it, because, even if you don't want me any more, I still want you, my darling. That hasn't changed. That's *never* changed. Neither am I entirely convinced I don't do anything for you any more in a sexual sense. Your eyes have always betrayed your feelings, and the way you were looking at me out at Lightning Ridge reminded me of how you used to look at me when we first met.'

'I won't deny I still find you physically attractive, Nathan,' she bit out brusquely. 'But lust without love has never appealed to me. Oh, I know you think I never really loved you, but that's your problem, not mine! *You're* the one who can't really love, not me. You obviously find sex an end in itself but I, for one, would find it repulsive.'

'Is that so?' Nathan said with seeming indifference. With equally seeming indifference, he reached out and picked up her nearest hand, turning it over and drawing it slowly up to his lips, his eyes narrowing as they locked on to her own wide, startled ones. 'In that case you'll find this repulsive,' he rasped, and sent his tongue-tip across the sensitive skin of her palm.

A shiver of sensation rippled up her arm and down through her body.

'And this...' He pressed the palm hard against his hot open mouth, exerting an inward sucking pressure as his tongue continued to go round and round on her wet, tingling flesh.

Everything inside Gemma clenched down hard.

God!

She kept telling herself to tear her eyes away, to tear her hand away. Instead, she remained frozen while those wicked eyes told her without words what he'd really like to be doing to her. Her mouth went dry as her memory provided her with plenty of arousing images. He was so good with his mouth. So very, very good. As for his tongue...there wasn't an inch of her body that it hadn't explored, making her shudder with pleasure.

She shuddered now.

'Come home with me,' he muttered into her hand, his voice thick with arousal. 'You won't regret it. I promise...'

He'd chosen the wrong word with 'regret'. For she would regret it. Bitterly. Her pride would suffer, and so would her self-esteem. She would be back on that merry-go-round to nowhere, back to being Nathan's sexual puppet, back to dancing to the strings he pulled. As much as she wanted to go with him, oh, so desperately, she could not. She *would* not!

Slowly, with her heart and body aching, she shook her head, till he stopped doing what he was doing and lifted his mouth from her hands. His expression was oddly bewildered.

'Why not?' he growled. 'You want to. I know you do.'

'Oh, yes,' she agreed. 'I want to, so badly it's almost painful.'

'I could make you,' he warned darkly, the glittering of raw desire in his eyes.

'No, you couldn't,' she said with surprising confidence. 'Not any more. Not without being as evil as Damian was. And you don't want to be like that, Nathan. I know you don't. Basically, you're a good man.'

He stared at her for a moment, clearly taken aback by her unexpected conviction. '*Am* I? I wonder... Would a good man do what I once did to you?' he said, squeezing her hands so tightly that she almost cried out. 'Would a good man ask you to get rid of his baby? Would a good man be trying to seduce you knowing that underneath you hate and despise him?'

Gemma didn't know what to say to that, her eyes wide upon his tormented face. Suddenly he released her hands, throwing them back into her lap with disgust in his gesture. 'You're still too trusting,' he snapped. 'Don't trust me, Gemma. Don't ever trust me. I'm not fit to be trusted.'

'You're frightening me, Nathan,' she whispered shakily.

'Good,' he snarled. 'Fear will keep you on your toes and on your guard.'

Now she was hopelessly confused, for along with the fire he'd managed to kindle in her veins was a feeling so much like love that it terrified the life out of her. She wanted to reach out to him and comfort him, to draw his tortured face down on to her breast and tell him she forgave him for everything.

Which showed that he was right. She *was* still too trusting. But at least he'd given her fair warning that his lust for her remained intact, and that he wouldn't hesitate to try to slake that lust when and if she gave him the chance. She would heed that warning and take the necessary steps not to be alone with him any more than was essential.

'In that case I don't want you dropping in on me unexpectedly up at Avoca,' she said crisply, her cool composure a total sham. But he didn't know that.

'Fine,' he said curtly.

'And I don't want you offering to drive me up there. I'll drive my own car.'

'Sensible.'

'I suppose I'll have to let you drive me home to Belleview tonight,' she muttered. 'It would look odd if you didn't. I dare say I'll have to stay there for a day or two before moving on. Ava will be angry with me if I don't.'

'No, she won't. She's not there. Belleview's deserted.'

'*What*?'

'I presume you know Byron and Celeste will be away for another two weeks cruising the Whitsunday Islands.'

'Yes, they wrote to me about it. They also said they were planning on selling the yacht up in Queensland at the end of their holiday then flying back. But I presumed Ava would be holding the fort at Belleview while they were away.'

'Well, she isn't. She got fed up with being in such a big house by herself and has moved into some luxury penthouse with Vince till Byron and Celeste return. Actually, Byron told me he was thinking of selling Belleview in the New Year. Celeste doesn't want to live permanently in the same house he lived in with Irene, and come February Ava will be married, which rather leaves the old place strapped for inhabitants.'

'What a shame,' Gemma said rather sadly. 'It's such a lovely house. It should stay in the family. What about Jade and Kyle? Maybe they'd like to live in it. They can't stay living in that houseboat after their baby is born, surely.'

'Byron offered it to them but Kyle recently bought a house in Castlecrag, overlooking the harbour. After living right on the water like that, they said they couldn't bear not to be near it. In truth, I don't think Belleview held too many happy memories for Jade but she didn't like to hurt her father by saying so.'

Gemma frowned. 'You seem well acquainted with the family's comings and goings. Have you been welcomed back into the fold?'

'Oh, I wouldn't say that exactly, but Byron keeps me informed. I haven't had that much to do with them, really, other than at Celeste and Byron's small wedding party.'

'What does everyone think is the situation between us?'

'Aah, now, you'll have to ask the individuals that yourself. It's not a matter I have discussed with anyone. I think Ava hopes we'll get back together again. She actually smiled at me. Once.'

'And what about Jade?'

'Jade, the dear romantic girl, has always thought we belonged together.'

'She also thinks you *love* me,' Gemma reminded him bluntly. 'And that I love you,' she added with a catch in her throat.

'Yes, well, Jade always was inclined to optimism,' Nathan drawled. 'I gained the impression she believes that given time you'd forgive me. Once she finds out you're pregnant, she'll be doubly sure.'

'Does...does everyone have to know that I'm pregnant?'

His sidewards glance was sharp. 'Why shouldn't they know? Are you reconsidering having an abortion?'

'Of course not!'

'Then there's no point in keeping it a secret. You having a baby will also put your returning to me into perspective as well.'

'I'm not really returning to you.'

'You know what I mean. Everyone will think you have. I'll tell them you're staying up in Avoca for the peace and quiet because you haven't been all that well, and that I visit you all the time. They won't know if it's true or not. Of course, I'm sure to have to bring Kirsty up to visit you on the occasional weekend, especially with summer on our doorstep. You know how much she loves the beach.'

'Oh, no, you don't! I recall what happened the last time the three of us were up there together. You dispatched Kirsty to an all-night movie session so that you could... could...'

'Have my wicked way with you?' he suggested drily.

'Yes,' she hissed, her mind filling with images she would rather have forgotten.

Nathan sighed a wistful sigh, as though he too were remembering. But any regret he was feeling was that he could not have a re-run this very night. 'I have to admit you've always been one hell of a temptation for me, Gemma.'

She didn't say anything to that. She didn't dare. What woman didn't want to be one hell of a temptation for a man? He couldn't have said anything more seductive if he tried. Oh, God, any minute now she would throw herself into his arms and beg him to take her home to bed.

'I can see you think I'm a right bastard,' he ground out. 'The kind only a mother could love.'

At this he laughed, the sound so dark and diabolical that the most horrible thought entered Gemma's mind. No, she denied quickly. Surely not! She couldn't have been that wicked. *Could* she? Gemma had read of such things but it was mostly a case of a father with his daughter, or perhaps a brother with a sister.

Yet she supposed it was possible for a mother to sexually abuse her son. It would explain Nathan's problem with really loving and trusting a woman, his focusing all his relationships on sex, as well as his reluctance to ever open up to anyone, especially about his past.

Oh, God, if it was true...

Gemma's tender heart filled with emotion, torn by feelings of sympathy and sadness which she had difficulty handling at this vulnerable time in her life. The more she thought about this idea the more she became convinced it was the answer to the puzzle that was Nathan Whitmore. Had Lenore had similar thoughts? Was that why she'd told Gemma that to throw Nathan away would be to destroy him? Maybe she should talk to Lenore, try to find out more about this enigma of a man she had married.

'You know, Nathan,' she said, trying to sound nonchalant, 'you've never really told me much about yourself. Irrespective of whether we eventually divorce or not, you're the father of my baby and I think it's time you told me a little more about your growing-up years.'

Slowly she turned a seemingly innocent face to his, but his answering frown suggested he was wondering what the hell had brought this subject up. 'I don't think this is the time and place for a D and M, Gemma,' he drawled.

'A D and M?' she repeated blankly.

'It stands for "deep and meaningful",' he volunteered drily.

'Oh, I see. But why not? We've a couple of hours to go and flying makes me nervous. I thought you might like to take my mind off things by telling me some childhood anecdotes.'

'I doubt anecdotes about *my* childhood would make soothing chit-chat,' he returned caustically, reinforcing

Gemma's suspicions. 'I suggest you settle back and try to have a sleep. Once we hit Mascot we have a long drive through peak-hour traffic to Belleview. Unless, of course, you've changed your mind about coming home with me,' he added, flicking her a wicked smile.

She hadn't, her returning smirk making his smile turn wry. 'I didn't think so. Trust me to marry a girl with character and class. Still, our son or daughter will be grateful for his mother's excellent qualities since he or she has the disadvantage of having me as a father.'

'You've been a good father to Kirsty, Nathan, and you know it.'

'Perhaps, but we all change, Gemma. I'm not the same man who married Lenore. I'm not even the same man who married you.'

Gemma could not disagree with that. Once before, she'd thought of him as a dark stranger. And yet, if what she thought was true, many things might be explained, and understood, and forgiven. If only she could get him to open up to her, to tell her what had happened to him as a boy. If only he could learn to trust her, maybe he could also learn to love her. He still wanted her. She could see that. Maybe if they lived together again, if she let him make love to her...

No!

Her reaction was automatic and instinctive. Nathan had always used sex as a way to avoid true intimacy. By always keeping his relationships superficial and lustful, he never had to reveal anything of himself but his beautiful body and his undoubtedly masterful technique. If she slept with him again, she would never find out a single damned thing. Only by keeping their relationship platonic did she have a hope of drawing him out. Look how much he'd spoken to her even just now, on this plane. Would he have done so if she had melted at his first touch, if she had stupidly agreed to move back in with him?

No way. He'd even now be seducing her with his eyes and his words, keeping her body so aroused all the time that she wouldn't be able to think straight. It was his *modus operandi* for women who threatened to get under his skin. Keep them trembling with desire and wide-eyed with wonder lest they find out that a real human being with real feelings and real failings lay beneath the super-suave, super-slick, super-smooth façade.

Still, it wasn't easy to pass up what he could deliver. Gemma had been quite correct when she'd said she found the thought of lust without love repulsive. But that wouldn't be the case with Nathan, would it? If this flight had proved anything, it was that she still loved the man as much as she ever had.

It was extremely painful for her to put him in a position where he would undoubtedly continue to be unfaithful. If there was one thing she knew and understood about her husband, it was that he could not tolerate celibacy, unless he was writing, which he wasn't at the moment.

But she would do it! It might kill her but she would make the sacrifice if it meant she might ultimately bring about the miracle. Miracles, Gemma suspected, sometimes needed a little human help.

'And what does that look mean?' Nathan said.

'Look? What look?'

'Don't play dumb with me, Gemma. You know damned well what look. It's the sort of look you see a lot in a dentist's waiting-room.'

'Oh, that look.'

'Yes, *that* look,' he repeated drily.

'I was just thinking I would have to stay the night at Belleview alone.'

'If you want company, I'll stay with you,' he offered silkily.

'I'll just bet you would, but no, thanks, Nathan. I'm sure you're needed back at the theatre. The show must go on, you know.'

'Actually, I've organised someone to look after things for me tonight, so I'm quite free. I couldn't possibly let you stay in that great barn all alone, considering it's already been empty a couple of nights. Empty houses are ready targets for burglars. No, don't bother to argue with me. I insist.'

Gemma bit her bottom lip. Damn the man! But what could she do?

'Very well,' she agreed curtly. 'Just don't try anything, Nathan.'

'I wouldn't dream of it. Not within Belleview's hallowed walls. Actually, do you realise we have never—er—done anything there?'

Gemma blushed. She might not have actually done anything with Nathan at Belleview but she'd thought about it a heck of a lot when she'd been living there before their marriage. She would never forget the first night he'd brought her there, especially when he'd been teaching her to play billiards and he had leant over her from behind and curved his startlingly aroused body around hers. If Lenore hadn't come in when she had, God knew what might have happened.

God knew what might happen tonight as well, if Nathan had any say in the matter. He'd warned her not to trust him an inch. And she didn't.

'We won't be changing the status quo either,' she told him sharply.

'Spoil-sport.'

Gemma threw Nathan a disbelieving look. 'What on earth's got into you, Nathan? It's not like you to be so...so...'

'Crass?'

'Yes,' she snapped.

'It's called frustration, darling. I took one look at you in those short shorts and that skimpy top today, and my recently flagging libido went into overdrive.'

'Nothing about your libido, Nathan,' she pointed out ruefully, 'has ever been flagging.'

'Certainly not with you.'

'Do you think we could get off this subject?'

'If you insist.'

'I insist.'

'Very well, but I must have the last word. If you ever change your mind, darling wife of mine, then do please give me the nod. I'll be ready and waiting. Now lie back, close your eyes and relax. We've still got an hour to go before we arrive in Sydney.'

Gemma indulged in a silent groan. Relax! When every nerve-ending in her body was sizzling with sexual awareness? And what of tonight, when she would be so temptingly alone with Nathan in that great empty house with so many beds to choose from?

God, but this was a stupid idea of mine all round, she thought. How am I ever going to keep to my vow to keep our relationship platonic? How?

CHAPTER EIGHT

IT WAS nearly seven-thirty by the time Nathan's dark blue Mercedes turned into Belleview, gliding through the gates and smoothly following the semicircular driveway around the large lily pond before stopping at the bottom of the wide stone steps.

Gemma glanced up at the impressively façaded house with its white-columned portico and air of gentle Southern grandeur, a wave of sadness sweeping through her to think that this beautiful home would soon be passing out of the family.

'It seems a shame Byron's going to sell this place,' she said with a wistful sigh.

Nathan slanted her a thoughtful glance before a wry smile tugged at his lips. 'Do you remember when you first saw it, you thought it was like something out of a fairy-tale?'

'Well, I don't think that any more,' she returned, a little sharply. 'But I still think it's one of the most beautiful houses I've ever seen. The time I spent living here was very happy.'

'As opposed to the time you spent as my wife.'

Gemma dragged in a deep breath, letting it out slowly as she twisted to face Nathan across the car. 'I could have been *very* happy as your wife,' she said, 'if only you'd treated me like a real wife, instead of an expensive mistress.'

'Most women would have given their eye-teeth to be treated as I treated you, Gemma.'

Her sigh was rather sad. 'Then obviously I'm not most women. I've always thought of marriage as a partnership, where husband and wife were best friends as well as lovers, best friends who shared everything and had no secrets from each other.'

'You kept secrets from me,' he reminded her coldly. 'You were seeing Damian Campbell on the sly. I don't mean you were sleeping with him,' he quickly amended when her face flamed with indignation, 'but you were meeting him and not telling me.'

'I was not *meeting* him,' she denied. 'He spoke to me briefly at the ball, and I ran into him once in the street during my lunch-hour. Look, I'm not going to be drawn into defending myself over Damian. Clearly, I wasn't equipped to deal with so devious a devil as he proved to be, but I also did nothing with him that I'm ashamed of. If I didn't tell you about those two early meetings, it's because you were such a possessive and jealous husband that I didn't dare. Which is another thing I found hard to handle—your extreme jealousy. Husbands and wives have to trust each other, Nathan. Without trust, any marriage is doomed.'

'Tell me, Gemma,' he said quietly, 'did I do anything *right* during our time together?'

'You . . . you made love very well . . .'

His laugh was very dry. 'Clearly that wasn't enough.'

'No.'

'And it wouldn't be enough the second time round either, would it?'

'No.'

He said nothing for a few moments, staring deep into her eyes till she was forced to swallow. Only at the last second did she stop herself from licking suddenly dry lips, but they did fall a little apart, and her damned pulse-rate took off like a racing car revving on the starting line.

'We'll see, Gemma,' he said at long last. 'We'll see . . .'

She almost groaned aloud by the time he finally tore those merciless eyes away, unsnapping his seatbelt and climbing out of the car. There was no doubt this was going to be a long and difficult night. But she was not going to waver from her resolves. Making love was out! No matter what he said or did. He could climb stark naked into her bed and she would simply turn the other cheek.

Gemma started to giggle at this last thought, and was still giggling when Nathan wrenched open her door. 'I must have missed the joke,' he said testily. 'Care to share it with me, since you're so large on sharing?'

Gemma pulled a face at him as she climbed out. 'Sarcasm doesn't become you, Nathan.'

'Neither does celibacy.'

'I haven't condemned you to celibacy. There are plenty of other fish in the sea.'

'So there are, my love. So there are. But fishing is such a tedious occupation.'

'Then go to a fish shop,' she countered caustically.

Nathan gave her a disbelieving look. 'Are you suggesting that I frequent a brothel?'

'I'm not suggesting anything,' she snapped. 'Your sex life is *your* problem, not mine. Now would you kindly get my luggage out of the boot? I'm tired and I'm hungry and I'd like to go inside.'

He blinked at her autocratic tone, not to mention her uncompromising stance. 'Is this the same sweet, accommodating girl I married?'

'You'd better believe it, buster,' she told him, feeling more in control of her life than she had in a long time. She had successfully deflected Nathan's sexual overtures with a suitable amount of style and sophistication, and was even capable of ordering him around without quivering afterwards. Her miracle still seemed a long way off, but she had a funny feeling she was on the right track. Turning, she marched up the steps to wait for Nathan near the front door.

'I don't think your stay out at Lightning Ridge has done you any good,' he grumbled as he did indeed extract her suitcase from the boot of the car and carried it up the steps, placing it at Gemma's feet while he unlocked the door. 'That Ma is a tough old bird, if ever I saw one. She threatened me that if I did the wrong thing by you again she was going to personally come down and flay every inch of flesh from my body with a bull whip, starting on my appendages.'

Gemma laughed. 'Good for Ma. There again, she might have to stand in line. After me I think maybe Celeste and

Kirsty and Lenore might like to have a go at you. I wouldn't think Ava or Jade would be too forgiving, either, if you start blotting your copybook again. Maybe I should even call Melanie in England and ask her what a suitable punishment might be.'

Nathan adopted an expression of feigned terror. 'God, don't do that. That woman used to frighten the life out of me! I can only admire Royce for taking her on. There again, any fool who would drive Formula One cars for a living has no appreciation of danger.'

'Melanie was a very warm and misunderstood lady,' Gemma insisted, brushing past Nathan to go inside, clicking on the light switch as she went. Immediately, the huge crystal chandelier hanging from the vaulted ceiling flooded the spacious foyer with light.

'I've heard the same said about Lucrezia Borgia,' Nathan drawled. 'Er. . .' He hesitated, throwing her a hopeful glance. 'What bedroom do you want me to put your case in?'

'Very funny, Nathan. The bedroom I've always slept in when I stay here, and it isn't yours.'

'Can't blame a guy for trying,' he muttered, and trudged on up the stairs. 'Put some coffee on, will you?' he called back over his shoulder. 'And see what food you can rustle up for us?'

When she didn't answer he stopped, turned and smiled down at her with a sheepish look on his face. '*Please*?'

Gemma sniffed. 'I suppose, since I have to eat myself, I could cook for two as well as one.'

'Thank God for that,' he muttered and moved on up the stairs.

Gemma stayed where she was a moment longer, smiling softly to herself, then frowning. Where had all her anger gone to? And her anxiety over what Nathan's intentions were? Was she being naïve and trusting again, thinking he really meant to try to win her back, that he sincerely wanted to change? Was he genuinely sorry for all the pain he had put her through? What about Jody, and the other women he had obviously been with while she was away? Was he going to put them aside and show her by his abstinence that he cared enough for her to do without if he couldn't have *her*, his wife?

Gemma had no faith in this last part. Nathan was not a man to embrace celibacy, as he had already indicated. She had long suspected sex was an emotional as well as a physical release for him. That was why, when he was writing, he didn't need it as much, because then he was pouring all his emotions in his characters.

Gemma made her way towards the kitchen, switching on lights as she went, wondering how she might get Nathan to start writing again. It would perhaps solve her worry over refusing him sexually, yet not wanting him to go to other women. She was moving through the family-room, pondering this dilemma, when she heard a noise which sparked some kind of recognition in her, but didn't register properly till she heard it again.

It was a dog, whining piteously.

She glanced around, but could see nothing.

The sound came again, thin and heart-rending. Gemma moved swiftly across the family-room, pulling the cord that shot the heavy curtains back from the French doors that led out on the terrace. A huge dog, which looked like no breed she had ever seen before, shrank back for a second before coming forward and pressing its black nose against the glass. His large brown eyes looked up into hers and it whined again.

'Oh, you poor darling,' Gemma groaned. A very large ugly dog, it was also as thin as an escapee from a concentration camp. It looked like it had some Great Dane in it, but she suspected it was a crossbreed. Naturally, there was no collar around its neck. What person would want to lay claim to such a neglected animal? Clearly, it had been dumped, and had come in here, looking for food.

'Wait there,' she told the pathetic, sad-eyed creature, and raced for the stairs.

'Nathan! Nathan! Where are you? Come quickly!'

He rocketed along the upstairs hallway to virtually collide with her, his eyes panicky. 'What is it? What's wrong?'

'I need the keys. There's a dog outside, a poor starving thing. I have to let it in and find it something to eat.'

Nathan grabbed her firmly by the shoulders, his expression exasperated. 'A *dog?* You came screaming up here about some stray dog? I thought something dreadful had happened.'

'Something dreadful has happened,' she informed him breathlessly. 'Some awful person has dumped the poor thing, probably he grew bigger than they thought he would. You should see him, Nathan. He's so thin, and his fur's all scraggy, and... and...'

'And he's probably full of fleas,' Nathan finished drily. 'As for letting it in and feeding it, you're not going to do any such thing. If you do, it'll never go away. And then it *will* starve, since you're going up to Avoca tomorrow.'

She stared at him, eyes wide and disbelieving. 'But... but... I can't not do something. I just *can't*!'

'Yes, you can,' he said with a callousness that made her shudder. 'People do it all the time. If you ignore it, it'll simply move on.'

Ignore that pitiable whining? Turn her back on those sad suffering eyes? What kind of inhuman creature did he think he was? What kind of inhuman creature was *he*?

'Well, other people might do it all the time,' she huffed, 'but I *don't*!' Angrily, she shook his hands off her shoulders. 'I'm not asking your permission to do this, Nathan. Just give me the keys, please.' She held out her hand stiffly, her mouth pouting her reproach. 'As for going up to Avoca tomorrow, I'll simply take the dog with me.'

Nathan shook his head in total exasperation. 'Why do I have to be married to a woman who's not like most *people*, let alone most other women?' he grumbled, then sighed resignedly. 'OK, Florence, lead on and I'll follow with keys to the ready. I'll be interested to see this poor pitiful creature for myself...

'Good God, it's a horse!' he exclaimed on sighting the dog on the terrace. 'And just look at those teeth!' On seeing Nathan the dog bared his teeth at him, probably in fear.

'Oh, for pity's sake,' Gemma exclaimed, snatching the keys out of Nathan's hand and walking over to unlock the sliding glass door nearest the dog. 'If you're so frightened of him,' she snapped over her shoulder, 'then by all means stay where you are. I don't need any help. I've handled dogs a damned sight fiercer than this one!'

The door unlocked, Gemma wrenched it open, then wished she hadn't done it so abruptly, for the sharp movement had made the dog immediately skitter away into the shadows at the edge of the terrace.

'See?' Nathan said. 'He doesn't want to come in.'

She shot him a withering glance. 'What is it with you? Didn't you have a dog when you were a boy?' Immediately, she wished she hadn't said that. Of course he hadn't had a dog as a boy. When was he home long enough to have a pet as demanding and time-consuming as a dog?

'Can't say that I did,' Nathan admitted, thankfully not looking too annoyed at the question. 'I had some goldfish once but one of my mother's friends used to flick his cigarette ash in the tank and they soon departed to the great goldfish bowl in the sky.'

Gemma filed away that little piece of information into her 'Nathan' file for future reference. Really he'd told her more today than he had in nearly six months of marriage. 'What about Kirsty?' she asked. 'Didn't she ever want a puppy for Christmas?'

'Nope. She was quite happy with her pet rock.'

'A pet *rock*? I've never heard of such a silly idea.'

Nathan's smile carried a dry amusement. 'They were rather big around Sydney for a while. And very popular with parents. Pet rocks don't have big teeth and they don't require feeding.' He frowned over at her. 'What are you doing just standing there in the doorway? Aren't you going to go over and grab the damned thing?'

'I'm letting "the damned thing" get used to me first, and even then I won't be doing any grabbing.'

By this time the dog had sunk down on its haunches at a respectable distance, its soulful brown eyes darting warily from Gemma to Nathan then back again. Gemma decided to sit down on the doorstep, knowing this building up of trust could take a while.

'You go and start seeing to some food, Nathan,' she called over to him. 'I know Ava always keeps steak in the freezer and the microwave will defrost it in no time.'

'God, yes, I could do with a steak.'

'I didn't mean *you*, silly.'

Nathan's expression was rueful. 'I had a feeling you didn't but it was worth a try. Maybe I'll be able to find enough for us humans as well as Jaws there.'

Jaws growled ominously at the mention of what Gemma decided wasn't a bad name for him . . . considering. In all honesty, she had never seen teeth like it. His choppers put Blue's to shame.

Thinking of Blue brought a soft smile to her lips. Putting her elbows on her knees, she supported her head in her hands and adopted a highly relaxed pose. If she had learnt one thing in handling Blue it was not to make any sudden movements. Nor to expect Rome to be built in a day.

'I think someone might have frightened you,' she said conversationally. 'Still, you probably frightened the dickens out of them if you just showed up on their doorstep. But you're really just a lamb in wolf's clothing, aren't you?'

The dog crawled slowly towards her as she talked, his tongue lolling out of one side of his huge mouth. Gemma slowly lifted her head and let her hands flop down her shins so that the dog could sniff them if and when he got close enough. It took a while but soon he was nudging his nose against her fingers.

'You sure he won't bite?'

Nathan's sudden and rather snappy query from just behind her ear sent the dog into immediate retreat, snarling up at Nathan as he scuttled away. Gemma rolled her eyes as she twisted her head to glare up at her husband. 'Did you have to frighten him like that?'

'Is it my fault that underneath his killer equipment the dog's basically a scaredy-cat?'

'Takes one to know one,' she mocked.

Nathan smiled, and Gemma's heart flip-flopped. He was so endearing when he smiled like that. And so damned attractive. She looked away then stood up. 'No point my staying here with you hovering,' she said a little brusquely. 'Did you find any steak in the freezer?'

'Only rump and fillet.'

'That'll do. Jaws won't know the difference.'

'Rump and fillet steak? For a *dog?* Good God, I—' He broke off suddenly, a frown bunching his brows together. '*Jaws?*'

'That's his name. You gave it to him.'

'I *did?*'

'Uh-huh. Don't you think it's appropriate?'

'It sounds depressingly permanent. You still mean to take him up to Avoca with you, don't you?'

'Of course. He'll make a good guard dog in time.'

'Yes, I suppose so,' Nathan murmured. 'I didn't think of that. All right.' He brightened. 'You can take him.'

'Gee whizz, thanks.'

'How do you know he doesn't belong to someone?' he went on, ignoring her sarcasm.

'Does he look as if he belongs to someone?' she retorted. 'If he does, that someone isn't going to get him back, believe me.'

'You'll have to get him checked over by a vet.'

'No trouble.'

'And he'll need a collar and lead.'

'We could get one tomorrow when the shops open.'

'You're as stubborn as Ma says you are,' Nathan growled.

'And you'll be as cold a bastard as she originally thought *you* were if you don't go along with me on this.'

Nathan smiled his defeat, though it was a wry smile. 'Do you think Jaws would like his steak diced, or in strips?'

Gemma threw her arms around his neck and kissed him before she could appreciate the stupidity of her action. Immediately, his arms snaked around her waist, pulling her hard against him, his mouth taking hers in a kiss that was nothing at all like the spontaneous and grateful peck she had given him. As the pressure of his lips increased, her head retreated. So did her arms from around his neck till her hands were pushing against his chest.

But Nathan had always been much stronger than he looked, and with one outspread palm centred firmly in the small of her back he was able to use his other hand to cup the back of her head and keep her mouth captured beneath his. Before Gemma knew it, he had pried her lips open, and his tongue was sliding, hot and wet, into her mouth.

At this point, Gemma's struggle became more internal than physical as she battled to find all those good reasons she had formed in her mind for why she should not allow Nathan to make love to her. With the pleasurable sensations bombarding her at that moment, they now seemed not only irrelevant but masochistic. Why shouldn't she just melt against the man she loved and let him take her away into that wonderful erotic world that he had always been able to weave for her? All she had to do was close her eyes and allow him free reign to her body. He needed no verbal permission, no instructions. Her body language could tell him what he needed to know, which was she wanted this as much as he did.

Already her mind was racing ahead to that moment when she would lie naked beneath him, when the lips which were at present imprisoning hers would seek out all those sensitive places where the mere brush of them would make her breath catch in her throat. Her breasts, the inner flesh of her thighs, the very essence of her womanhood...

Her moan of surrender brought an answering groan from deep within Nathan's throat. Her hands were sliding up around his neck again, her thoughts having spun out into nothingness, when the cavalry came to her rescue in the form of a very large, very scruffy dog, who launched his trembling form through the open doorway and snapped his formidable teeth at the leg of the bad man attacking his nice new friend.

CHAPTER NINE

GEMMA'S arm flopped over the edge of the sofa where she had spent the night, her fingertips encountering something warm and furry. That something warm and furry also had a tongue like sandpaper.

'Yuk,' she shuddered, but refrained from whipping her hand away from the licking. Instead she opened her eyes and looked straight into a pair of beseeching brown eyes. 'Well, Jaws?' she said, rolling over on to her side and scratching him behind the ears with her other hand, the distraction stopping that icky licking. 'I suppose I should be grateful to you. So how come I'm not, eh? How come I'd like to get hold of your scrawny neck and wring it?'

Gemma said all this in a calmly smiling voice so that the end result was that Jaws lay there on the rug next to the sofa, happily thumping his tail from side to side. She'd always known it was the tone of voice, not the content of the words, that dogs responded to.

'Just as well you didn't really damage Nathan,' she told the adoring animal, 'or you wouldn't be here now. He'd have called the dog-catcher in so fast, you wouldn't have known what hit you.'

Jaws had fortunately only got a mouthful of trousers before Nathan wrenched away from Gemma and shouted at the dog, whereupon the poor creature, whose bravery was exceeded far and away by his cowardice, bolted back out on to the terrace. Nathan had scowled, slammed the door and turned back to Gemma. But the moment had been broken—thank God—and he'd quickly realised it, much to his frustration and fury.

'Not that you're popular,' Gemma told the happily pant-ing dog. 'I think you've been consigned to the Siberia of Nathan's mind. And believe me, that's a chilly place.'

The dog suddenly stiffened, then a low ominous growl rumbled in his throat. Gemma levered herself up on to her elbow and glanced over the back of the sofa. The door-knob leading out into the hallway was turning, and soon Nathan popped his head into the family-room. Jaws im-mediately leapt to his feet, quivering with outrage and fear.

'Would you kindly put that beast outside?' Nathan de-manded curtly. 'I'd like to have some breakfast.'

Gemma smothered a smile. 'Wait a sec. I have to put my dressing-gown on first.' No way was she going to swan around in her nightie, which was hardly neck-to-knee. She hadn't owned that kind of nightwear since she married Na-than, who had showered her with gifts of highly erotic lin-gerie from the very first day of their marriage.

She had, however, bought a simple cotton housecoat while staying with Ma, and it was this she drew modestly over the white silk and lace number which she'd slept in and which left little to the imagination. Once decently covered, she shepherded the dog outside, closing the door on her re-turn.

'You can come in now,' she called out.

Nathan came into the room, blue jeans and a white T-shirt on, blond hair still wet from a shower. He looked much more coolly composed than he had been when he'd stormed out of this same room the night before, Gemma thought as she followed him out to the kitchen, but just as lethally sexy. The sooner she got herself up to Avoca alone, the better.

'Sleep well?' she asked, deciding trite conversation was better than the tense silence that seemed to have suddenly enveloped the kitchen.

'Don't ask stupid bloody questions,' he snapped over the electric kettle. 'Of course I didn't damned well sleep well!'

'Oh...'

He glared at her, then down at the small hint of white lace that was in evidence across the base of the V neckline of the housecoat. 'I was going to make the magnanimous offer to drive up to Avoca in front of you today, since you're not familiar with the way, but after last night's fiasco I've decided against that idea.'

'Oh . . .' Gemma did her best to hide her disappointment but couldn't. Annoyed with herself, she looked down, wryly accepting that after last night her own resolve to keep their relationship platonic was wavering.

When she looked up again, Nathan's eyes had narrowed and he was searching her face with a ruthless scrutiny that unnerved her. 'If you want me to come up with you, then say so. If you want me to stay. . . I can easily do that too. The play's running like clockwork and I have an assistant director who can handle things for a while.'

'Whatever gave you the idea I would want you to stay?' she said, doing her best to sound surprised. 'Don't misinterpret what happened last night, Nathan. You kissed me and I momentarily kissed you back. I would have stopped it myself any moment if Jaws hadn't.'

He made a scoffing sound. 'You expect me to believe that?'

'Believe what you damned well like,' she retorted haughtily. 'I have no intention of going back on what I said. We only have a pretend marriage for now. There will be no sex!'

'I see,' he bit out. 'Well, in that case, I have no alternative but to take the necessary steps to see that I don't go stark raving mad!'

Gemma paled, but she lifted her chin bravely. 'I've already told you I don't expect you to live the life of a monk, but I . . . I hope you'll be . . . discreet.'

He stared at her. '*Discreet*? Is that all you care about, that I'm *discreet*?'

Gemma felt as if he was backing her into an emotional corner where any moment she would blurt out the truth, that of course that wasn't the only thing she cared about. She cared about *him*. She *loved* him. But her ultimate goal in all this was to win his love, not just his lust. She wanted the whole miracle and this was the only way she could think of to secure it. If that meant she had to risk his going with another woman for sex, then so be it. But that didn't mean she had to like it!

'For God's sake, what do you want from me?' she lashed out. 'You hurt me, Nathan. You hurt me badly. I can't just take you back into my bed like that. I need time. I need for you to prove that you care about me. I'm not just a body. I have feelings, in here.' And she thumped her chest. 'And I have a baby growing, in here.' Her hands dropped down to cross over her still flat stomach. 'This baby needs a father who respects its mother, who thinks of her as more than a bed partner.'

'I don't just think of you as a bed partner,' he said stiffly.

'Is that so? Then pardon me if I say your actions don't back up that statement. You've always given me the impression that all you've ever wanted from me was sex, even now, after all we've been through and with my having your baby. Oh, I know you find it a wonderfully safe topic and a wonderfully safe activity. And I think I understand why. It's such a marvellous escape. From everything. From the past, and the present and the future. When it's good, it can create a world where reality recedes. And when it's great, it can begin to become an end in itself, an obsession. Believe me when I tell you I could easily become as obsessed by what you could do for me sexually as you once were with me. But I can't afford that kind of escape or obsession any more, Nathan. I'm having a baby. I'm going to be a mother. I have other priorities now, such as stability and security. Prove to me that I can rely on your still being my husband and a good father to our baby till death us do part, and I'll give you all the sex you want.'

He said nothing for quite a while, simply stared at her with one of those closed-book faces he could wear and which always made her want to scream with frustration. 'That was some speech,' he said at long last, his voice low and coolly controlled. 'Just tell me one thing before I get the hell out of this house. Do you still love me?'

Gemma groaned silently. What could she say to that? She didn't want to lie but she didn't want to admit such a thing, either. It might negate all she was trying to achieve.

'You once told me you didn't believe I ever really loved you,' she hedged. 'So how can I *still* love you?'

He smiled. It was not a very nice smile. 'Don't play games with me, Gemma. I want the truth and I want it now.'

Gemma thought of something Ma had said and decided it was better than lying. 'How can you love someone you don't even know?' she successfully evaded again.

Nathan scowled at her. 'What in hell does that mean?'

'It means just that, Nathan. I don't know you, not the inner you, the real you. I don't know your secret hopes and wants and dreams. I don't know what has hurt you in the past, or why you do the things you do sometimes, or react the way you do. All I know is the superficial you, the flesh that covers your bones. Oh, it's very nicely arranged flesh and you certainly know what to do with it in bed. Maybe I'm still "in love" with that flesh, but do I love you, Nathan? I'm just not sure about that.'

And oddly, having said so, Gemma could see that what she said could possibly be true. Maybe her instinctive responses to Nathan were still bound up in the extremely strong physical attraction they shared. Maybe she didn't really love him. Oh, God, she felt so confused.

'Maybe I shouldn't have asked,' Nathan muttered, then lanced her with a piercing look. 'Are you sure you want this baby, Gemma? I can't stand to think of an innocent child suffering for something I did. I've never told you how dreadfully sorry I am for what happened that day. I have no excuse. What I did was unforgivable, but you...'

'Nathan, stop,' she said shakily. 'I *have* forgiven you for that. How many times do I have to tell you? If I gave you the impression out at the Ridge that I didn't want this baby, then I apologise. What I didn't want was for my baby's parents to be divorced, nor to have to bring up my child alone as a single parent. I know what that's like, as I'm sure you do, and it's hardly an ideal situation. But I would never make our child suffer for the way he or she was conceived. If I thought for a moment I might do that, I would have considered an abortion. But I never did. Not for a moment.'

'Thank you for that,' he said quietly. 'I really appreciate it. I was rather worried about that.'

'Then why didn't you say so before?'

'What?'

'Why didn't you tell me you were worried? It's what husbands and wives do, you know. Tell each other their worries.'

He seemed disconcerted by the idea.

Gemma decided they'd had enough heavy conversation for one morning. Nathan's system looked in danger of overload. 'Are you making coffee, or just standing there inspecting the kettle?' she quipped with a bright smile.

His eyes showed even more bewilderment, but after a bemused shake of his head he plugged in the kettle and set about getting out the coffee and the mugs.

'After breakfast,' she went on airily, 'I'll get you to draw me a map. And then I'm going to send you up the road for some dog supplies. After that I...'

Gemma kept him busy right up to the moment when he waved her and Jaws off. Actually, she felt quite nervous over the prospect of finding her way north up the highway to Avoca all alone—a distance of some eighty kilometres or so—but she didn't let Nathan see that. It was important to her that he see she could cope very well alone, that she was not some wishy-washy weak female who would go to mush at the first little problem.

Nevertheless, when it came right down to it, he'd still been loath to let her go, saying he was concerned over her living all alone, vowing to be up first thing the following Saturday with Kirsty in tow. Since it was already Wednesday that wasn't all that far away, but as Belleview and Nathan receded into the distance behind her it suddenly seemed like an eternity to Gemma.

The drive turned out to be very tedious, what with Jaws refusing to lie down on the back seat, spending the whole time standing up with his huge head hanging over her seat, dripping saliva down her back. Clearly, he had never been taken in a car before, the excessive panting a sign of extreme nervousness. And while Gemma tried to be patient with him, it was very distracting and tiring.

On top of that she got lost a couple of times. Well, not exactly lost, but she sailed past two turnings she was supposed to take before realising it, having to then negotiate difficult U-turns and double back before getting herself on to the right roads. She was very relieved finally to roll into Avoca and know she was only a couple of minutes away from the beach house.

Gemma glanced over to the ocean on her left as she drove slowly along the narrow main road that wound through the small seaside town. It being a Wednesday in the last week of November, with school holidays still a couple of weeks off, it wasn't very busy. But that would all change soon, she realised. The Central Coast was a popular holiday haunt for Sydneysiders, sun, surf and sand drawing them like magnets. Avoca was only one of a host of beach towns up this way, but it was one of the most popular, boasting plenty of white sand, good board-riding waves and a relaxed, laid-back life-style which beckoned stressed office and factory workers, especially over the Christmas break.

Gemma had not been up this way at Christmas, having only come to Sydney from Lightning Ridge last February, but she'd spent Easter up here and if that was anything to go by Avoca was about to become a hive of activity. In a way, she wasn't looking forward to it, her stint back up at the Ridge having made her appreciate peace and quiet. Still, she didn't have to leave the house if she didn't want to. It was spacious, with its own pool and a huge front balcony with a magnificent view of the Pacific Ocean.

The old picture theatre that was the pride and joy of Avoca came into view, signalling to Gemma that she was now only seconds away from home. God, but she would be glad to put her feet up and have a nice cool drink.

'And I'll be glad to get you off my back, dog,' she told Jaws, who responded by giving her another one of those huge icky licks on the face. 'Don't do that!' she said sharply, then immediately felt sorry when the dog slunk back. 'I'm sorry, Jaws, come back and lick me all you like. Yes, that's right. Good dog, good dog. No you're not a good dog,' she went in the same soothing voice, smiling through gritted teeth while he slobbered all over her. 'You're a smelly, skinny, flea-bitten excuse for a dog who'll probably be more trouble than you're worth but I guess I'm stuck with you now, even if you are the ugliest, most oversized, undernourished, scrawny, scraggy pooch I have ever set eyes upon.'

Jaws responded to her well disguised lambasting with a resounding 'Woof woof' which almost blew her ear drums.

'Good God,' she muttered as she swung the car into the steep driveway that led up the side of the house and into a car-port. 'I suggest you keep that bark for emergencies, Jaws. If the neighbours get a load of it too often, I'll be arrested for noise pollution.'

Getting the dog out of the car was almost as difficult as it had been getting him in. But once actually on terra firma again, he stopped dragging back on his lead. Gemma was happy to deposit him in the thankfully fully fenced back yard, leaving him with a good supply of dry dog-food and a big bowl of water before she got on with opening up the house. It clearly hadn't been used for some time and smelt a little musty.

Apparently, whenever Nathan wanted to use it, he would contact a local cleaning lady who came round and aired the house, putting a duster and vacuum cleaner through the place before he arrived as well as stocking up the kitchen cupboards and refrigerator with essentials. But Gemma had vetoed his doing that this time. She would have little enough to do if someone started doing the housework and shopping for her. She'd also told Nathan she would make it her business to contact a pool-cleaning service and get the pool into swimming condition. Apparently, it hadn't been used this summer as yet and was green with algae.

Gemma had barely unlocked the front door and let herself in, thinking the unloading of the car could wait till she'd been to the toilet and had that cool drink, when the telephone started ringing. She just knew it was Nathan before she'd heard a single word.

'Yes, Nathan, I'm here safely,' she said straight away.

'How did you know it was me?'

'Extra-sensory perception?' She couldn't help a little teasing. 'Come on, Nathan, who else could it have possibly been? Who else knows I'm even back from Lightning Ridge, let alone up here at Avoca?'

'I could have rung Ava and Jade and told them.'

'Did you?'

'No, because then I'd have to explain why you were up there and not down here with me.'

'I thought you were going to say I hadn't been well...'

'Lord, can you imagine what reception that would get? I'd be accused of all sorts of negligent behaviour then given the cold-shoulder treatment again. No, Gemma, if you don't mind, I think I'll keep your presence up there a secret for a while yet.'

'You won't be able to keep it a secret from Kirsty if you're going to bring her up with you on Saturday.'

'I was rather hoping you might change your mind about that and let me come up alone. I promise on my word of honour that I'll be a good boy.'

The road to hell was paved with good intentions, Gemma thought drily. And Nathan wasn't the only one who might lapse. She recognised her own weaknesses where he was concerned only too well.

'Gemma?'

Her sigh was resigned. How could she refuse him entirely when he'd been so sweet, when it was obvious that he cared about her and was worried about her? But that didn't mean she had to do something as stupid as sleep alone with him in the same house he had first seduced her in. The vibes would be against her from the start.

'All right, Nathan. But I don't want you to stay the night. What if you come up just for the Sunday? I'll cook you a nice Sunday roast.'

Gemma could tell by his silence that he was disappointed with her answer but she wasn't going to budge.

'Thank you for the generous offer,' he said a touch testily, 'but if I'm only going to have your company for one day, I don't want you cooking. I'll book us somewhere nice for lunch up there.'

Better and better, she thought. A public place was infinitely safer than a private kitchen. Nathan had done things in the kitchen of their apartment in Elizabeth Bay which showed he needed neither a bed nor night time to put his desires into action.

'How's Jaws?' he asked abruptly. 'He didn't look too settled as you drove off.'

'He was a right pain in the neck all the way,' she admitted. 'But he's fine now.'

'You should have let me take him to the RSPCA,' he grumbled.

'Now, Nathan, you know no one would choose a dog like him. He's too darned big and too darned ugly. He'd have ended up being put down.'

'I suppose so,' he sighed. 'Well, I'd better get myself down to the theatre and see what's been going on in my absence. No doubt there'll be some minor calamity.'

'I thought you said your assistant director could handle things.'

'I lied.'

She laughed.

'I'll ring you tomorrow,' he insisted, 'see how you're faring.'

'Don't worry if I'm not in. I have vets to see and shopping to do.'

'And you have to go to a proper doctor, don't forget, get yourself a referral to a obstetrician up that way.'

'I'll do that, Nathan. Don't fuss.'

'I'm not fussing.'

'You are so too. Now say goodbye and hang up, will you? I have heaps to do.'

'You sure know how to make a man feel wanted,' he muttered.

Gemma was glad he couldn't see her face. Dear lord, she wanted him like mad. Thinking about those kitchen antics they had got up to on occasions had not had a good effect on her. Sunday, she already suspected, was going to be hell!

'Hang up, Nathan,' she ordered in a monotone as she clenched her teeth.

'All right, damn you, I will!'

CHAPTER TEN

GEMMA found the next few days living totally alone—except for Jaws—a real surprise. She'd always thought of herself as a bit of a loner, having never had a close girl-friend during her school years, having in fact spent many, many long hours of her young life by herself.

So she really hadn't expected to find living alone any great trial, or for it to require any major adjustments.

But she soon realised that she had never spent twenty-four hours, straight, alone, and never at night. By Friday night, she'd brought Jaws into the house, even allowing him to sleep on the end of her bed.

Yet for all the dog's company she still felt lonely for human contact. She found herself talking for longer than strictly necessary to the vet, to the doctor, to shop assistants, even a bank teller. Nathan's telephone calls were real life-lines and she tried to keep him talking, but he was not a chatterer. Once he had reassured himself that she was all right, he would ring off. In that respect he hadn't changed.

So by Saturday she was really looking forward to the next day and Nathan's visit. Any risk to her sexual resolves were secondary to her desperate need to see someone she knew, and who knew her. Gemma also finally accepted that she was bored, and would have to find things to do to fill the long lonely hours. Because if she didn't, she would surely weaken and move back to Sydney to live with Nathan.

Nine o'clock on Saturday morning saw her driving to Erina Fair, the largest shopping centre on the Central Coast and only ten minutes from Avoca. Gemma spent a lovely few hours finding and buying something attractive and summery to wear to lunch the next day, then splurging out totally on a new sewing-machine, some maternity patterns and some material. On top of that, she bought a selection of blockbuster novels. Then, on the way home, she dropped into the local video shop and joined up, brought home a couple of comedies to watch that night. Laughter was good medicine for loneliness and boredom. Or so she'd read somewhere.

When she arrived home, Jaws went off his brain with excitement, barking that great woofing bark of his as he leapt up and down at the side gate as if he were on a pogo stick. Gemma hoped he hadn't been doing much of that while she was away or the neighbours would soon be complaining, although the high wooden side fences plus the thickly foliaged trees which grew along each boundary provided a good sound barrier.

To make up for her absence, she made a big fuss of the dog, opening a tin of special dog-food, after which she let him into the house, where he soon settled down on the rug in front of the television in the main living-room. Gemma spent the next couple of hours setting up the sewing-machine on the dining-room table and learning its various intricacies. She'd taken textiles and design as a subject at school and was a good sewer, but had made little use of her talent since marrying Nathan. He'd chosen most of her clothes, dressing her in designer labels, seeming to know what looked best on her hour-glass figure. Once, he'd even gone as far as to have a balldress specially made for her from his own design.

Gemma cringed a little as she thought of that dress. Because thinking of that dress inevitably made her think of the ball, which had been the occasion of her first meeting with Damian. She really hadn't come to terms with Damian yet. Was he born bad, or had he become bad? Had he perhaps been corrupted by someone at a crucial point in his young life?

Gemma began to wonder what his relationship had been with his half-sister, Irene. She had undoubtedly been a twisted personality with a great capacity for hate and revenge. Had she got hold of Damian as a youngster and warped his mind to her own wickedly selfish way of looking at life?

Gemma's thoughts slipped from Damian to Irene without missing a beat. What had really happened between Byron's wife and Nathan? She no longer believed Nathan had slept with her. But he must have done something to make Irene lie so viciously about him. Maybe she had made a play for him out of some kind of revenge for Byron having had an affair with Celeste, and he'd scorned her advances. That seemed to fit in with what she knew of both of them. Maybe she would ask Nathan about it tomorrow...

If she dared.

Gemma rose from the dining-table with a frown on her face. Thinking about people like Damian and Irene always agitated her, maybe because she was afraid that in some small way Nathan was like them. Gemma was a simple, straightforward person, happy to say openly what she thought and felt. Dealing with dark and complex personalities such as Nathan's was not easy for her. She hated the feeling of not knowing exactly what she was dealing with, of being unsure.

Yes, she would ask him about Irene tomorrow. And she might ask him about other things as well. His mother, for instance...

Gemma gulped. Well, maybe not.

Six that night found her sitting in front of her television watching the news and devouring a home-made hamburger and chips. Any guilt over the cholesterol content was justified by saying she was eating for two. In truth, her recent stay in the heat of the outback had steamed a few pounds off the body. She was very streamlined, except for her breasts, which had gone from her normal B-cup to a C. The doctor she had visited this week had assured her this was perfectly normal and that she was lucky to have good-sized nipples, as a lot of fuller-breasted women sometimes had surprisingly small nipples, which made breast-feeding a problem.

Well, there was nothing flat about *her*, she thought drily. She would probably have enough milk to feed quads! Some girls at school had envied her her bust but quite frankly she'd always thought her breasts an embarrassment and a nuisance.

Still, Nathan seemed to like them. A lot.

Gemma thought of the outfit she had bought for her lunch date with him tomorrow and experienced a stab of guilt. If she wasn't prepared to sleep with the man, why tease him? And that green and white polka-dot dress was a definite tease, being halter-necked, with a built-in bra that moulded and lifted her breasts into a cleavage that would have made Marilyn Monroe look under-endowed. Of course, it did have a small white bolero jacket which hid most of the curves and which she planned on wearing. But there would still be a hint of that eye-catching cleavage on show.

Gemma had made the decision not to wear the damned dress after all when suddenly Nathan's face appeared on the television screen before her. Startled, she stopped eating mid-chip, mouth agape when the camera panned to bring into focus the blonde whose arm was cosily linked with his and who was also smiling up into his handsome face with a sickeningly sweet smile.

'I'm so excited,' she was simpering. 'When Lenore decided out of the blue to leave the play come Christmas, I never dreamt I would get the lead role. But darling Nathan has faith in me, and I can only say I will do my level best to reward that faith in me.' This last little gem of gratitude was accompanied by a look that no one could mistake. It had 'I'm yours, darling, as often as—and in any way—you want me' written all over.

Before Gemma could stop herself she threw what was left of her plate of chips at the screen and leapt to her feet. 'You lying bastard!' she screamed. 'You're sleeping with that whore and now all the world knows it!'

At her explosive tirade, Jaws had jumped to his feet as well, whimpering with confusion before stopping to gobble up the chips that were gradually sliding down the television, dropping one by delicious one on to the floor.

'Traitor,' she snarled at him, then slumped down on the cane sofa and burst into tears.

Don't jump to conclusions, a tiny little voice tried to re-assure her, but without much success.

'This isn't a jump,' she sobbed aloud. 'It's a tweenie weenie step!'

She wept noisily and angrily, but her hurt and her anger eventually turned into a full-on blaming of herself.

What did she expect him to do when she'd rejected him and virtually given him permission to be unfaithful? Nathan was not a man to go meekly to bed every night without the comfort he obviously found in a woman's body. She had been a fool to think he wouldn't. And a fool to think that when he did she wouldn't feel like killing him.

Because she did. She wanted to get in her car right at this moment, driving down to Sydney and scratch his eyes out. As for blondie—nothing was too good for that slut! Gemma fantasied about superglueing her lips together, so that she wouldn't be able to perform, either in that play or on other women's husbands!

She's only giving him what you never would, that awful little voice said again.

Gemma groaned admission of this. How many times had Nathan subtly suggested she take a more aggressive role in lovemaking, only to have her shrink away like a blushing virgin? God, what a fool she had been! What a fool she still was, pushing Nathan away in the one area where they were compatible. They could be even more compatible if she could get over her squeamishness when it came to certain activities.

No, it wasn't squeamishness, she realised as she pondered the problem. It was more a lack of confidence. When Nathan was making love to *her*, she would spin out into another world, but it was a world of mindless receiving, not giving. If *she* started making love to him, she would be taking responsibility for *his* pleasure. It was a daunting thought. What if she was no good at it? What if, when one came right down to it, she was a fumbler and a bumbler? What if she lacked the courage to go through with whatever she started?

By this time Gemma was pacing the room, Jaws trailing behind her. Around and around the lounge they went, till Gemma suddenly ground to a halt, looking down at the dog with some amusement at the picture they would have presented to an outsider.

'This is a damned silly way to take you for a walk!' she pronounced, then laughed. 'Come on, I'll get your lead and we'll go for a real walk, then I have some deciding to do.'

Sunday dawned with the promise of a hot summer's day. November had slid into December in the few days since Gemma had seen Nathan, and with it the weather had been consistently fine and warm. Beach weather. Only Gemma was not overly fond of the beach, or at least not the surf. Having been brought up in the outback, she found the sea intimidating. Nevertheless, she'd come to quite like walking along the sand, and even around the rocks when the tide was out and there were no crashing spraying waves to frighten her.

Nathan had said he would arrive no later than eleven-thirty, but it was nearly noon by the time his Mercedes pulled into the driveway. Gemma, who'd been fully made up and dressed by eleven, was hopelessly agitated by this time.

'You're late,' she snapped, glaring down at Nathan over the balcony railing as his golden head appeared out of the car.

He glanced up at her, grey eyes lazily amused. 'And hello to you too,' he drawled. 'I really like the "I'm so glad you've arrived safely—did you have a nice trip?" greeting.'

For all her determination to be cool and sophisticated about the Jody situation—she had resolved not even to mention it—Gemma suddenly found herself seething with jealousy and a desire to say something cuttingly pointed. She controlled that urge, but was still left with a sour disposition.

'I was worried,' she complained crossly.

'There was an accident on the expressway which held things up for a while,' he said as he strode around the car to mount the steep front steps. 'And I'm not that late, Gemma.'

'You should have started out earlier,' she told him waspishly. 'Or did you have a particularly late night?'

This last remark brought a sharp look. 'No later than usual on a Saturday night. There's always extra curtain calls on a Saturday night.'

He reached the top of the steps and Gemma allowed herself to look at him, *really* look at him.

For a man in his mid-thirties, he had no right to look so damned good, she decided. He still had all of that thick golden hair, he wasn't carrying an ounce of flab, and any lines on his face only seemed to enhance his looks, rather than detract in any way. Dressed as he was today in dark grey trousers and open-necked, short-sleeved shirt in the finest cream lawn, he looked no older than thirty and every inch a man other women would throw themselves at.

Gemma's eyes travelled back up his body again finally to meet puzzled eyes. 'Is my fly open or something?' he said.

She tossed her head somewhat irritably. 'No, I was just thinking how well preserved you were for a man of thirty-five.'

'God, you make me sound like a bottle of pickles,' he said ruefully. 'And I'm not thirty-five any more, either. I had a birthday a couple of weeks back.'

Gemma looked stricken.

'Now don't start going all sentimental on me,' he went on impatiently. 'I've never set much store by birthdays. Only children get hurt when people forget their birthdays. Adults don't give a damn.'

But I'll bet you were hurt often as a child, Gemma thought. I'll bet that drug-addict mother of yours forgot your birthday more times than I've had hot dinners.

'I've made a booking for twelve-thirty,' he continued, 'so we might as well get going straight away. It's gone noon and, while it'll only take a few minutes or so to get there, it'll take an eternity to find a parking spot at this time of day on a sunny Sunday.'

'Where are we going?'

'The Holiday Inn at Terrigal.'

'Oh, good, I haven't been to Terrigal yet. I hear it's very nice.'

'I would say it's the prettiest place I've ever seen. I'd have bought a house there if the surf were better. Speaking of pretty...' He looked her up and down, his eyes finally settling on her cleavage. One eyebrow arched, before his eyes lifted back to hers. 'I was about to say that was a very pretty dress you're wearing but I doubt the word *pretty* is adequate. Where did you get it? I don't recall seeing it in your wardrobe before.'

'I bought it yesterday.'

'With our lunch date in mind?'

Gemma quivered inside, both with apprehension and excitement, but it was too late to go back now. She looked him straight in the eye. 'Yes,' she said simply, and with that word told him all he needed to know.

Yet his reaction was odd. His grey eyes darkened to slate, narrowing thoughtfully on her face. Oddly enough, she didn't think he was really looking at her face. His mind seemed to be somewhere else.

'What are you thinking about?' she said, her snappy tone jerking him back to the present.

The hint of a sardonic smile pulled at his mouth. 'I was thinking I should have brought Kirsty with me.'

It came to Gemma then that he didn't realise she meant to go through with it. He probably thought she was just teasing him. Or maybe *testing* him. So before fear—or a lack of confidence—could set in she walked forward, wound her arms up around his neck, went up on tiptoe and kissed him.

His lips felt startled and stiff under hers at first, neither did he make any attempt to put his arms around her, so she tightened her own grip, leant fully against him, then sent her tonguetip forward as he had often done to her, stroking his lips till they groaned apart.

Up till that moment, Gemma had been rather cool and calculating in what she was doing, but the split-second she actually slid her tongue forward and into his mouth an incredible explosion of raw desire mushroomed up through her, taking her by surprise. Her moan was the moan of naked passion, as was the way her tongue started moving, darting deep into his mouth again and again in a feverish echo of what she suddenly wanted his flesh to be doing inside hers.

Her senses leapt when she felt his hands on her, spanning her tiny waist and squeezing it. She welcomed his roughness, loving the feel of his fingertips digging into her skin. Till suddenly he was lifting her away from him, her mouth wrenched from his quite violently.

'No, Gemma,' he said in an astonishingly composed voice.

She started up at him, aware of her hot tingling mouth and her hot tingling body, aware of herself as a woman in a way she never had been before. How could he be so calm when she wanted to tear the clothes from his body, wanted to *devour* him, wanted to do all those things she had never wanted to do before?

'Why not?' she groaned. 'I don't understand...' Her eyes dropped away in the confusion and misery of acute frustration.

'Because you don't really want this,' he said starkly.

Big brown eyes flew upwards. 'My God, how can you say that? Did you think that was *acting*?' The word 'acting' catapulted the reason for Nathan's control into her mind with the sting of a scorpion's tail. Reefing herself away from where his hands had been resting lightly on her waist, she scowled her disgust at him. 'I know why you don't want to make love to me,' she spat. 'You don't need to after screwing dear old Jody into the early hours of the morning.'

His pretend shock made her doubly angry. 'Oh, don't bother to deny it,' she flung at him. 'I saw you both on television the other night and I saw the way she was looking at you, not to mention what she *said*. One didn't have to be a genius to put two and two together. I stupidly blamed myself for forcing you into the arms of another woman but now I see that's where you'd prefer to be. God, she must be good! Or is it that dear old inexperienced Gemma is just so pathetically boring? Well, maybe I can find someone who doesn't find me so boring. Maybe I'll go find myself an ego-booster as well!'

For a few seconds, Nathan's face turned a ghastly shade of grey but then he rallied, his expression one of apology and concern. 'If you got the wrong idea with that inter-view, Gemma, then I am deeply sorry. What can I say ex-cept to repeat that there is nothing between Jody and myself on a personal basis? Nor any other woman for that matter. There has been no other woman for me but you, since the first day we met.'

'Pull the other leg, Nathan,' she scorned. 'It yodels.'

His eyes went hard and flinty as he battled for control. 'I'm trying to be patient with you—and with Jody, in a way—because I realise the initial fault was all mine by act-ing with her the way I did at the party, then taking her home afterwards. I had every intention of sleeping with her that night. I admit it. But I knew, the moment she walked into our apartment and sat down in *your* chair, that I couldn't do it. I gave her a drink, told her I was sorry and called her a cab.'

'Then why did she act like she was your mistress to the television interviewer?'

'She'd still like to be. She'd like to be the mistress of any man who could do for her career what I could. She's a very ambitious actress. She also happens to be a very good one. So when the opportunity presented itself, I gave her what she wanted in the hope that she wouldn't keep chasing me. Un-fortunately, she hasn't got the message yet, but I'll be a lit-tle blunter in future. On top of that, come January, the play moves on to Melbourne and I'm not going with it.'

'You're not?'

'No. I've had a gutful of directing. I'm going back to writing.'

'Oh?' Gemma's heart leapt at this news. It was what she had wanted him to do, knowing how involved he got when he wrote. No way would he look at another woman once he had his nose buried in the computer screen. 'A new play, or that old one you have trouble with?'

'A new one, I think. I have a story in mind, full of conflict and erotic promise.'

'Sounds good. What's it about?'

Nathan's smile was mischievous. 'It's about a man who's married to a beautiful young girl many years younger than himself, and whom he's completely potty over. But things begin to go wrong and they become estranged for a while. She thinks he only wants her for sex, you see, and she won't have him back till he proves to her that his feelings run much deeper than that. He's dead determined to do just that, even though she makes it pretty hard on the bloke by wearing these seductive clothes and doing stupid things like French kissing him in the middle of the day.'

'Really? How inconsiderate of her!'

'That's what the husband thinks. He needs to prove to her, you see, that he can control himself in that regard, because he did something once... something that made him weep with remorse afterwards.'

At his confession the bleakest clouds gathered in his eyes and her heart turned over. 'Oh, Nathan,' she murmured, her own eyes filling with tears.

When her tears seemed to perturb him greatly, she quickly blinked them away and summoned up a smile from somewhere. 'Enough talk of plots and plays. If we don't leave soon, we'll be late for lunch. I'll just go put Jaws out the back, then get my jacket and purse.'

He brightened at this. 'That dress has a jacket?'

'Yes.'

'Thank heaven for small mercies!'

CHAPTER ELEVEN

NATHAN was right about Terrigal. Gemma agreed that it had to be one of the prettiest places in the world. The beach itself was delightful, curving round to end in a small protected cove which Nathan told her was called the Haven. She could see what he meant by the surf, however. Its waves were rather gentle and more suited to family enjoyment than daredevil board riders.

There was no shortage of families that day, a myriad umbrellas and bodies dotting the white sands, and many more sitting on rugs under the stately Norfolk pines which shaded a grassy area at the edge of the beach.

Opposite these pines stood the majestic and quite magnificent Holiday Inn, whose Mediterranean architecture made one think of the French Riviera. Not that Gemma had been to the Riviera, but she had seen plenty of pictures. And Terrigal, she fancied, would not be misplaced there, especially with the way the hills hugged the shore, houses built all over the steep hillsides to take advantage of the panoramic view.

Nathan drove slowly down the main street past the hotel, then turned a couple of corners that took them round to what looked like the back of the hotel but which, as it turned out, housed the main entrance.

'My God, a parking spot!' he exclaimed, zipping the Mercedes into a space between two cars. 'Wonders will never cease. You must have brought me good luck, Gemma. This never happens when Kirsty is with me. We always go round and round the block for ages, then end up parking miles away and having to walk.'

'We can only stay here for two hours,' she warned him, looking up at the sign as they both climbed out.

'I think we should manage to finish lunch in two hours, don't you?'

'I should hope so, provided the service isn't too slow.'

Nathan slid his arm through hers. 'Didn't I tell you? It's buffet-style. You serve yourself. And you can go back for more as often as you like.'

'Mmm. Sounds marvellous. But very fattening.'

'You could do with some fattening up. You've lost weight.'

'Not from everywhere,' she said drily.

His eyes slid down to the deep valley between her breasts. 'Yes, so I noticed.'

'You're making me blush,' she chided.

'You're making me do a few things too.'

'Nathan, stop it.'

'Can't, I'm afraid.'

'What . . . what are you going to do?'

'Steer you through these revolving glass doors, with you firmly in front while I try to think of other things and hope for the best.'

Gemma was so busy trying to keep a straight face as Nathan did this that she didn't initially appreciate the cool spaciousness inside the hotel, or its quite splendid décor which was oddly Victorian, rather than Mediterranean.

'Keep going,' Nathan said through gritted teeth and urged her past Reception and up a wide staircase which divided into two at the first landing, sweeping left and right in semicircles up to the first level, where signs indicated various restaurants and convention rooms. Gemma also spotted Ladies' and Gents' rest-rooms.

'You could always go to the Gent's for a while,' she whispered to Nathan.

'I'd rather go the Ladies',' he growled. 'Look, let's just lean over this railing for a minute or two, then I should be all right.'

They did so, in silence, Gemma pretending to look around, all the while torn between laughter and a touch of lingering guilt. If she hadn't been wearing such a revealing dress, Nathan wouldn't be in the awkward situation he was in right now.

Yet it was really his own fault, wasn't it? They could have been, at this very moment, back at the beach house, in bed. This was what he had chosen to do. In a way, she was almost enjoying his discomfort, which was rather wicked of her. But justified, she imagined. My God, she had suffered a lot at this man's hands. Shouldn't he suffer a little?

'Right,' he said testily after a full five minutes. 'Let's go in now.'

'Which way?'

'Right behind you.'

It was called the Conservatory, being a largely glassed-in area with huge windows overlooking the beach, and a glass ceiling which had some kind of protective shade-cloth draped over it, probably to keep the heat down. Perhaps such a design would have been better suited to an English hotel rather than one in sunny Australia, Gemma thought, though it was spectacular to look at.

The smorgasbord menu was arranged on tables to the left and right as one walked in. Gemma was agog at the splendid array of dishes, both hot and cold. Everything looked mouthwateringly appetising.

'Down this way, Gemma,' Nathan directed, taking her arm and practically dragging her away from the food and down the steps that led into main body of the restaurant. Nathan gave his name and a waitress led them over to a table next to one of the windows—one of the few empty tables left.

Gemma was happy to see that the atmosphere was casual. There weren't even tablecloths, their small circular table having a black marble top of which the cutlery setting was directly arranged, the green chairs equally casual and countrified with wrought-iron arms, wooden slats up the back and cushions to sit on.

Once seated, Nathan ordered a glass of Riesling for Gemma and a light beer for himself.

'We'll have a drink first, shall we,' he suggested, 'before getting up to select our first course?'

She nodded her agreement and was content to wait for their drinks in silence, admiring the view of the pines below and the beach beyond. The water was a deep blue-green under the bright sunshine, the sky a softer blue than an outback sky.

'It's so beautiful here,' she murmured at last.

'I'll bring you here to stay some time,' he offered.

She smiled. 'Yes, I'd like that.'

Though the food proved as delicious as it looked and the ambience very relaxing, the next two hours provided absolutely no opportunity for Gemma to have anything approaching an in-depth conversation with Nathan. Their table was not far from three other tables, one on either side and one behind. Anything she said could easily be overheard, so, in the end, all they talked about was what they ate, or what Gemma's plans were for filling in her time up at Avoca alone.

'You don't have to make your own dresses, you know,' Nathan said over his dessert. 'I'm sure there are boutiques in Sydney which specialise in individually designed maternity wear. I could bring you down to Sydney one day and buy you all the outfits you might need.'

Gemma counted to ten. 'I *like* sewing, Nathan,' she said firmly.

'Then make baby clothes,' he ordered. 'I don't like the idea of my wife wearing home-made clothes.'

'I'm only making things to wear around the house,' she said with a sigh.

'Is it a crime to want my wife to have the best?' he asked. 'Besides, it gives me pleasure to see you wearing beautiful clothes.'

'I'm not a dress-up doll, Nathan,' she reproached.

'Oh, I see,' he snapped, angry now. 'This is another of the many things I did wrong as a husband. I bought you beautiful clothes. God, what a bastard I am to do such a terrible thing. Do forgive me for being generous and wanting to make you happy.'

Gemma groaned before putting down her spoon and staring blankly out at the horizon, a weariness seeping across her mind. Would Nathan never see that *things* didn't make a wife happy? When she said as much, he scowled. Gemma looked away in disgust.

'Does it hurt to let me give you things,' he went on irritably, 'if it makes *me* happy? And who knows, maybe there are some things I can give you which *will* make you happy?'

Her expression became exasperated as she turned back to face him. 'Such as what? There's only so much clothes and jewellery a girl can wear. She can only drive one car and live in one house at a time. Everything else is sheer extravagance and indulgence. I wasn't brought up to riches, Nathan, and while I do like to be comfortable—who doesn't?—I do not need to have luxuries lavished upon me to be happy.'

'I see...' He began playing with his dessert, clearly put out by her answer. Had he already been planning more presents in an attempt to win her back?

She reached over and covered his hand with hers, stilling it. 'You've already given me one of life's most precious gifts, Nathan,' she said softly. 'A baby...'

He winced, then glanced up at her, that old cynical gleam in his eyes. 'I'm still to be convinced you're thrilled about that,' he said curtly.

Gemma's hand withdrew on a gasp of shock, her own face growing hard with hurt. 'Then that's your loss, Nathan. I'm not going to try to convince you of it.'

'No...no, I don't suppose you are,' he said agitatedly, then glanced around till he attracted the waitress's attention, asking for coffee and the bill in the same brusque voice. Ten minutes later saw them walking in frozen silence back to the car. Once they were both seated, Nathan threw her an exasperated look.

'For God's sake, don't go giving me the cold shoulder,' he growled. 'I don't want to go back to Sydney with you being angry with me when I've been doing my damnedest all day to do the right thing by you.'

Gemma wearily shook her head. 'I'm not angry, Nathan. More frustrated. You just don't see so many things.'

'But I *am* trying. And perhaps there are things *you* don't see. You're not perfect, Gemma. Stop demanding perfection in return.'

She stared at him. Was that what she was doing? Demanding perfection?

His suddenly tender smile scattered her already confused thoughts. 'You must realise, my love,' he said gently, 'that you don't have all the answers to life, because you haven't lived all that much of it yet. You are looking for a Utopian existence which no man worth his salt can give to you. Men and women are by nature very different individuals. They don't always complement each other. Sometimes they clash. You want me to pour out my soul to you, but I don't feel comfortable doing that. You'll have to learn to trust me without knowing the ins and outs of every moment of my life before I met you.'

'I don't want to know the ins and outs of every moment of your life before you met me,' she argued. 'Just a few crucial ones.'

'Such as?'

'Such as what happened between you and Irene? What *really* happened?'

'Aah ... so Damian wins, does he? The bastard is dead, but you still believe him and not me.'

'No! I *did* believe you when you told me you didn't sleep with her. But I'm not a fool, Nathan. Something else happened. Maybe I'm just being a typical female but I can't seem to get it out of my mind. I need to know.'

'And if I tell you, my love, what else will you need to know, I wonder?'

Her mind flashed to his mother and she coloured guiltily. Luckily, Nathan wasn't looking at her at that precise moment. He had leant forward to start the car and was even now easing it away from the kerb, looking over his shoulder to the right.

'I will tell you if you insist, but don't blame me if you don't like what you hear. I don't pretend to be a saint, even today, but this happened many, many years ago, at a time in my life when I had little pity for women, and none at all for a certain type.'

Gemma gulped. *Did* she want to hear this?

Nathan glanced over at her but it seemed her curiosity was greater than her fear, for she said nothing.

'I knew from the first day I came to live at Belleview,' he began as he drove home, 'that Irene was the biggest two-faced bitch of all time. She was absolutely vile to Ava, vicious to Jade, but sweet as apple pie to Byron. I dare say she did love him in her own warped way but it was plain to anyone with a brain in their head that he didn't love her back. Oh, he tolerated her remarkably well, but there was no real warmth in his dealings with his wife, and certainly no passion.'

'How could there be?' Gemma remarked. 'He was in love with my mother, with Celeste.'

'So it seems. But he hadn't had anything to do with her for some considerable time, so I have no doubt Byron slept with his wife when he was at home. I doubt, however, that she ever felt that she'd been "made love" to. Consequently, she hated anyone or anything she believed took Byron's love away from her. Celeste. Ava. Jade. All of them had been victims of her jealousy. When Byron adopted me, she pretended to be all for the idea, whereas in truth she was violently jealous of me as well. I think she decided to seduce me as a kind of revenge for Byron not loving her. On top of that, I think she may have been titillated by what Byron had told her of my lifestyle when he first met me.'

'What...what lifestyle was that?' Gemma asked tentatively.

Nathan's laughter was mocking. 'Come now, you mean Ava hasn't already told you of my living with some woman old enough to be my mother? I find that hard to believe.'

'She...may have mentioned it.'

'I'll bet she did. And it's true,' he added quite ruthlessly. 'Lorna was forty-two when I moved in with her, while I was a tender sixteen. Since my own mother had only been thirty-three when she died, that made Lorna more than old enough to fulfil a parental role if that was what she wanted. And there was a degree of mothering in the way she treated me . . . at first.'

Nathan chuckled darkly and Gemma swallowed.

'But the circumstances of my eventual deflowering are hardly relevant to the story of Irene and myself,' he went on savagely, stunning Gemma with this revelation. 'Deflowering' suggested he'd been a *virgin* before moving in with this Lorna person.

Before she could stop herself, her eyes snapped round, wide and shocked. 'But I thought—' she blurted out.

'Thought what? That Lorna couldn't possibly have been my first? That with the sort of upbringing I had, I must have had plenty of opportunities for sexual experimentation before that?'

'Yes,' she said in a small voice, though inwardly relieved that the horrors she had been imagining were not true.

'Oh, believe me, I had scores of opportunities. I was a well grown lad by the time I was fourteen. My mother's friends starting coming on to me around that time. And I don't mean just her women friends.'

'But you resisted them?'

'Yes, I did—surprise! surprise!—despite some of the women being quite young and very sexy. One or two were almost as beautiful as my mother who, believe me, was something to behold, despite her drug-taking habits. She was like a golden goddess, with long blonde hair and a body men would kill for. Yet it was her aura that drew them like magnets, that irritatingly innocent aura which made them think she couldn't possibly have been humped by as many men as she had.'

Gemma cringed at his crude words but said nothing to stop the outpouring.

'God, but she was a promiscuous bitch! I can't remember a time when I didn't lie in my bed at night and hear her with some creep in the next room. Do you know what it's like to hear your mother moaning and groaning like that, Gemma? Can you imagine how I felt, lying in my little bed, forbidden to come out of my room but worried sick that she was actually being hurt? And then, as I grew older and I knew damned well what was going on, I would lie there, hating her. And hating the excitement it gave me listening to my own mother...'

'Oh, Nathan...'

'Don't get me wrong,' he snarled. 'I loved her too. And she loved me. She used to put me in boarding-school when she was involved with anyone who wasn't nice to me. It was her way of protecting me, yet all I wanted to do was protect *her*, so I would run away and make trouble for whatever bastard was screwing her at the time and he would ultimately leave. Then, for a while, we would have a great time together, till another jockey came on the scene.'

He stopped to scoop in several steadying breaths, Gemma moved to tears for the boy who must have been in torment most of his childhood. But at least he hadn't been abused as she had feared he might have been. His mother had loved him in a fashion, and he had loved her, which meant he was capable of love, capable of giving his heart, even to an unworthy recipient.

'You know, I'll never believe she overdosed deliberately,' he went on. 'She wouldn't have done that. It was probably an accident. Someone must have given her some heroin that was stronger than she thought it was. Hell, when I found her dead that day I was devastated. I cried and cried, and then I went out and got roaring drunk.'

'And is that when you got tangled up with Lorna?' Gemma suggested softly. 'When you were at your most vulnerable?'

He nodded, slowly, wryly. They were not far from Avoca at this stage and suddenly, Nathan pulled over to the side of the road and cut the engine. Inside the car became deathly quiet except for Nathan's ragged breathing.

'She was a friend of my mother's,' he grated out. 'One of the only women who had never come on to me. I thought I was safe with her. And I was, for a while.' He gave a low, dark chuckle. 'I had this fantasy, you see, that I would stay a virgin till I fell in love and married. I guess that's what happens to boys with mothers like mine. They either become just as promiscuous, or they do the exact opposite. I had always vowed I would never be like my mother. What a naïve young idiot I was! One night, Lorna showed me what a fool's paradise I was living in. Boy, did she ever show me.'

His cold laughter left her stunned and speechless.

'Damian didn't try an original technique with you, my dear,' he continued caustically. 'Using drugs to turn a person on against their will is hardly new, especially when combined with alcohol. One night my devious den-mother got me drunk then gave me an added little something. I must have passed out because when I came round I was lying spread-eagled and starkers on her bed, where she proceeded to show me that sex with a woman you didn't love was far from repulsive.

'Admittedly, at first, I was not altogether comfortable with what was happening to me. My mind kept saying no, but all the while my body just kept on saying yes. I even bawled like a baby when I couldn't help coming under those rapacious lips and hands. Yet any remorse did not stop my youthful body from becoming aroused again within minutes, neither could I find the will to stop her from taking me as if I was nothing but a thing to be used, over and over and over.'

Gemma's whole mouth had gone dry with the tale, her eyes wide, yet her mind racing with new and understanding thoughts. My God, doesn't he know he wasn't to blame for any of that? What that evil old bitch had done had been tantamount to rape!

Yes, of course he realised that, she accepted with the dawning of wisdom, which was why he was so appalled at himself for raping *her*. And why he was so worried about her having anything to do with the likes of Damian, who had no conscience where women were concerned. She had been as sexually naïve as Nathan had been back then, both of them ideal victims for unscrupulous and debauched people like Lorna and Damian.

Nathan broke into her train of thought with a dry laugh. 'I can see the cogs of your fertile and forgiving brain working, Mrs Whitmore, but don't whitewash me totally yet. I went on living with Lorna well after the drink and the drugs wore off. She taught me everything I know about sex, the conniving corrupting bitch, and I enjoyed every damned moment. You also don't know what I did to Irene, which I knowingly and deliberately planned and executed.'

Gemma bit her bottom lip as everything inside started churning ominously.

'Well you might look worried,' Nathan said ruefully. 'Are you sure you have the stomach for the rest of this? You're looking a little green around the gills.'

Gemma lifted her nose and her chin. 'I want to know *everything* about you, warts and all!'

'Do you, now? Well, don't say you weren't warned!' he laughed. 'It's not a pretty story and I have no intention of watering it down. Irene came to my bedroom one night a few weeks after my adoption. It was very late, Byron was away on business, and she was wearing a very transparent négligé. Have you ever seen a photograph of Irene when she was younger, Gemma? No, you wouldn't have. That vain bitch got rid of all her early photographs when her looks began to go. She was extremely attractive and very sensual, with black hair and eyes, and a tall voluptuous figure. Let me assure you that nearly twenty years ago she looked very enticing in that sheer gear.

'If she was nervous, she didn't show it. She boldly stood with her back against the door and told me that if I didn't do what she wanted she would tell Byron I had made indecent advances to her while he was away. Given my background I naturally thought Byron would believe his wife, not me, and that I would be thrown out on the streets. She then went on to tell me what she wanted, and I felt sick with shame and fear.'

'Well, of course you did!'

Nathan's sidewards glance was withering. 'Not because of what you're thinking. Because I was so damned tempted! Lorna had done her job very well. I only had to look at Byron's near-naked wife and I was immediately stunningly aroused. Fortunately, I had a dressing-gown on over my pyjamas and Irene didn't notice. But this time, my respect for Byron was far greater than my desire for his wife. I hit upon a plan which I hoped would stop her in her tracks and guarantee that she would never tempt me again.'

'What . . . what did you do?'

'I told her I would be only too happy to do what she asked and that I thought she was the most beautiful, sexy, desirable woman in the world and that I hadn't been able to think of doing anything else except making love to her since I arrived at Belleview. Then I told her that Lorna had taught me an oriental technique which would intensify her pleasure. I explained to her that if we delayed our lovemaking for twenty-hours, during that time anticipation of what was to come would heighten her arousal to such a pitch she would never forget the experience.'

'Good lord!'

'Is that an exclamation of shock-horror or interest at the technique?' Nathan drawled.

'I . . . I—er—um . . .' She licked dry lips. Which *was* it?

'Never mind,' he snapped. 'I made it up, but it sounded plausible enough. I needed time to get my equipment together.'

'Equipment?' Gemma squawked.

'Not *that* equipment. I had to get my hands on a tape-recorder.'

'A tape-recorder . . .'

'That's right. I hired one from a local rental shop, put in a blank tape and hid it under the bed. When the time approached for my rendezvous with Irene, I turned it on. She showed up five minutes later. With great difficulty, I talked her into just sitting on the side of the bed while she told me in lurid detail everything she wanted me to do to her, and everything she was going to do to me. I convinced her this was part of the technique, and if she had enough grit to wait one more night without release the experience would blow her mind. The next day I had copies of the tapes made, one of which I gave to her, explaining what was on it and that if she ever came near me again I would give a copy to Byron. In a sudden inspiration I also told her if she laid a hand on Jade again the same thing would happen.'

'What...what was her reaction?'

'She cried. She ranted and raved. She begged me, then cursed me. In the end, she just seemed frightened of me. I have to admit I took great pleasure in her fear. I had never had anyone afraid of me before and I like the feeling of power, of being in control. I vowed to remain in control of my life—and my sexuality—from that moment on.

'By and large I have kept that vow. Only once...' he slid a black glance her way '...did I lapse, but I don't have to tell you about that, do I? In fact, I think I've told you far and away too much already. I dare say you'll try to psychoanalyse every damned thing I do from this moment on. You do have a tendency to want to analyse the whys and wherefores of my behaviour. In that respect you're very much like your father. Byron used to probe endlessly about my past when I first met him. Thank God, he soon gave up that idea and let me get on with my life. Now it's time for us to get on with our lives, Gemma, which means I'd better start up this car and get you home. The afternoon's sliding away and I still have several things to discuss with you.'

'Such as what?' she asked a little distractedly, her mind whirling with all Nathan had told her.

'Such as exactly what story we're going to be telling Byron and Celeste. I received a call last night saying they had a buyer for the boat but the man wants to take possession immediately. They're flying home tomorrow.'

CHAPTER TWELVE

THE moment Celeste arrived in Sydney and found out about Gemma's pregnancy she was up at the Avoca beach house as if she'd been shot out of a cannon. Byron was with her, but of course his attitude was one of smug satisfaction, whereas Celeste could not hide her concern underneath her congratulations, so much so that soon after their arrival Celeste contrived some errand for Byron to do down the road so that she could be alone with her daughter.

Gemma was left to face her mother with some trepidation, knowing Celeste was sure to ask her all sorts of awkward questions, including the one Gemma did not want to answer. In fact the moment Byron left Celeste launched forth.

'So what's going on here, Gemma?' she asked bluntly. 'I don't believe all that garbage Nathan fed Byron about you and he being totally reconciled, and that you were both thrilled about the baby. If that's so why aren't you living with Nathan down in Sydney? And I certainly don't believe his excuse that you were staying up here because you'd been feeling poorly and the sea air was good for you. You look as fit as a fiddle to me. Blooming, in fact.'

'Well, I ... I—'

'For pity's sake don't feed me waffle,' Celeste interrupted impatiently. 'Just give it to me straight. I can't abide people beating around the bush. I love you, darling, and I'll stand by you, no matter what, but I must know the truth.'

Gemma knew that any hope of either hedging or colouring the situation differently had been well and truly dashed. Celeste would spot her lies a mile off because she knew too much. Not for the first time, Gemma regretted having told her mother about that incident with Nathan. But she had, and nothing was going to change that.

'Nathan and I *are* having a sort of trial reconciliation because of the baby,' she answered matter-of-factly. 'But I didn't want to live with him because I'm not sleeping with him at the moment. I want to see if he can learn to care for me as a person, not just a bedmate. And yes, for your information only, the baby *was* conceived on that afternoon at Campbell Court. And no, that doesn't bother me one iota. I want this baby and I will love it as much as I love its father.'

Celeste's eyebrows shot up at this. 'I thought you hated him!'

Gemma's smile was wry. 'Now, Mother... coming from you, that's almost funny. How many years did you go round saying you hated my father?'

'Mothers don't want their daughters to be as dumb as they've been,' Celeste grumbled. 'Loving Byron gave me many years of heartache.'

'And many years of happiness... from now on.'

Celeste nodded slowly. 'I suppose so. But that's because Byron loves me back. Can you say the same for *your* husband?'

'No. Not yet. He wants to love me, I think. He's just not sure how. But he's trying, Celeste. He's trying very hard. And he's talking to me, telling me things he would never have told me before.'

'Really? I'm surprised. Nathan has never struck me as a confider.'

'No, he's not. Normally. But I've been able to get him at a vulnerable moment or two when he said more than he intended. Not that he tells me everything. Often I have to try to fill in the missing pieces and sometimes I'm way off beam, but I'm getting there. In time, I think I'll be able to put the complete puzzle which is Nathan together. He had a very rough childhood, you know. He needs a lot of understanding and compassion.''

Celeste frowned. 'You had a rough childhood too, Gemma. Everyone's had a rough something or other at some time in their lives, but in the end you have to go forward, not back. Don't probe too deeply, love. Maybe there are things you're better off not knowing. And maybe there are things you'd be better off doing.' So saying, she gave her a sharp look. 'You're *really* not sleeping with him?'

Gemma tried not to blush. 'No.'

'And he's going along with that?'

Gemma recalled his rejection of her offering herself on a silver platter and an embarrassed heat gathered in her cheeks. 'Yes, he is,' she said staunchly, which brought another disbelieving look from her mother.

'He's not still sleeping with that Jody woman, is he?'

'He never did sleep with her.'

'Is that what he told you?'

Gemma could not help smiling at her mother's cynical scepticism. 'Yes, that's what he told me and I believe him because he didn't have to give me any such reassurance. I'd already told him he could sleep with other women if he wanted to.'

Celeste blinked her astonishment. 'Good God, are you *crazy*?'

'Yep. Crazy about him. So crazy I'm prepared to do just about anything to win his love.'

Celeste was shaking her head. 'Dear girl, I think I will have to tell you the facts of life where men are concerned. You never *ever* give them permission to sleep with other women. They're likely to take you up on the offer.'

'Nathan won't.'

Celeste threw her hands up in the air. 'The girl's gone bonkers!'

'You don't know Nathan.'

'And I aim to keep it that way.'

'He told me he didn't think too badly of you any more. In fact, I think he rather admires you.'

Celeste stared at her daughter, her cat's eyes narrowing. 'Are you conning me?'

'Never!'

'Hmm. I suppose I might have to try to get along with him too, now that he's fathered my first grandchild.'

'Yes, Grandma,' Gemma teased.

Celeste grimaced. 'Gosh, that sounds awful, doesn't it? I'll be forty next week too. I'm getting old, Gemma,' she wailed.

'The only thing you're getting,' her daughter returned, 'is more beautiful every day. Marriage suits you.'

Celeste flushed with pleasure. 'Really? You think so? I...I've put on a bit of weight lately. All that lazing around on deck and drinking champagne.'

'Sounds blissful.'

'It was,' Celeste sighed.

'So why sell the boat?'

'Oh, it wasn't the silly boat that was blissful,' she said dismissively. 'It was...' She broke off, her eyes flying to her daughter's. For the first time, possibly in her entire life, Gemma imagined, the outrageous head of Campbell Jewels looked embarrassed.

'Mother,' Gemma said laughingly, 'what have you and Daddy been up to?'

Daddy chose that precise moment to return, a flagon of sherry in each hand. He stood outside on the front balcony, tapping one of the flagons against the sliding glass doors and mouthing for them to let him in. Gemma did so, giving him an all-encompassing glance as she did so. Golly, but he was looking fantastic. Tanned and relaxed and very youthful. No one would believe he was fifty. From Celeste's reaction, he hadn't been acting as if he was fifty, either.

'And what are you grinning at, daughter? Or maybe I shouldn't ask. Been talking about me behind my back, have you?' he threw at both of them as he walked over to put the flagons on the counter separating the kitchen from the living-room.

'Couldn't find the brand you asked for, Celeste,' he went on, reaching up to slide back the doors of the glass cabinet above the counter and bring down three glasses. 'The man in the bottle shop said he thought they stopped making it back in 1922, so I bought these two instead. He recommended them as similar in taste. One's cream sherry and one's sweet.'

'Thank you, darling,' Celeste purred, knowing full well that the brand she'd asked for didn't even exist. It had simply been a ploy to keep Byron busy while she'd questioned Gemma.

'Let's have a tipple, then,' Byron went on expansively, opening the cream sherry and filling the three glasses. 'Later I'm going to take my two lovely ladies out to dinner.'

'You don't have to do that,' Gemma protested. 'I can cook, you know.'

'My dear,' Celeste said with a rolling-eyed glance of exasperation, 'if a man offers to take you out to dinner then don't object. Truly, I think I need to take you in hand in matters concerning the opposite sex.'

Byron gave Celeste a look that could only be classified as *classified*!

'I think we'll leave Gemma's education in the opposite sex up to Nathan, don't you?' Byron drawled. 'And speaking of Nathan, he told me to tell you he'd be up on Friday night.'

'F...Friday night?' Gemma stammered.

'Yes. And so will Jade and Kyle. Nathan's invited them for the weekend.'

'Oh...' Gemma didn't know whether to be relieved or worried. Wouldn't Jade and Kyle think it odd if she and Nathan slept in separate rooms? Or didn't Nathan intend sleeping in a separate room? Maybe he'd changed his mind about that...

'How nice for you to have company,' Celeste murmured, her knowing eyes telling Gemma exactly what she was thinking. 'You must get lonely all week up here without Nathan.'

'Actually, I quite like living alone,' she said swiftly. 'I'm used to it.'

'Is that a hint for us to leave?' her father asked.

'Not at all! I'd be horribly disappointed if you didn't stay a couple of days at least.'

'Good, because we're going to. We both planned to be away from our respective offices till the end of the week, didn't we, Celeste? So we'll stay up here with you till Friday, then pass you over to Nathan and Co. Now come over here, both of you, and get your sherry.'

'A hundred dollars you don't make it through the weekend without succumbing,' Celeste whispered to Gemma as they walked over to the counter.

Gemma was startled at first, then amused. Selecting the nearest sherry, she lifted it to her lips, meeting her mother's dancing eyes over the rim of the glass. 'Make it a real bet,' she whispered back as soon as she got the chance. 'Or aren't you that confident?'

'Will you ladies excuse me a moment?' Byron said. 'I'm going to take my sherry out by the pool and say hello again to that great dog of yours, Gemma. I can see now how he managed to get over the fences at Belleview. Never seen such a big dog in all my life, but I like him.'

'Go right ahead. I'm just glad he likes you back.'

'Oh? Has he been vicious with anyone else?'

'Only Nathan so far. And I wouldn't say vicious. But it's daggers drawn every time they meet. Jaws doesn't try to bite him any more, but he still growls a lot.'

'But he took to me right away,' Byron said, sounding puzzled.

'He liked the pool-cleaning man too. I think it's just Nathan.'

'Whatever did he do to the dog?'

'Nothing, really. I think maybe Jaws is a frustrated guard dog and he seems to think I need guarding from Nathan.'

'Smart dog,' Celeste muttered under her breath, but fortunately Byron didn't hear as he made his way out of the room.

'So what was Nathan doing to you,' Celeste asked with suspicion in her voice, 'that made the dog think you needed protecting?'

Gemma sighed. 'Don't jump to conclusions. He was only kissing me.'

'There's kissing and there's kissing, daughter, dear. I presume you were trying to fight the bastard off and he wasn't responding.'

Gemma laughed. 'I wasn't fighting at all and *I* was the one who was responding. Jaws has my undying gratitude for intervening.'

'Aah, so Nathan *isn't* happy with this "no bed" rule you've made.'

'I never said he was *happy* about it.'

'Just as I thought! You haven't got a chance of holding out against him for a whole weekend, Gemma, not when you're in love with the man. I hope you realise that.'

Gemma shrugged. 'As I said, I'm willing to bet on it.'

'All right. How much *do* you want to bet?'

'You decide, since you're so sure of my capitulating.'

'All right. If I lose, I'll give you the Heart of Fire...'

Gemma's mouth dropped open, her hand freezing around her sherry glass. Celeste had paid two million dollars for the Heart of Fire. Gemma had once coveted the magnificent black opal, had indeed thought she had inherited it for a short while. She'd been badly disappointed when she'd found out it was stolen property. She could still remember the first moment she'd turned it over in her hand, and been captivated by its rare splendour.

Would the chance of really owning that priceless gem be enough to stop her from making love with Nathan if he changed his mind and set his sights on seduction over the weekend? Gemma doubted it.

'And if I lose?' she asked.

Celeste's smile was quite smug. 'If you lose, I get to name the baby.'

Gemma blinked her surprise at such an ill balanced bet.

'I...I never got the chance to name you, you see,' her mother explained, a wealth of emotion in her voice and her face.

A lump immediately formed in Gemma's throat. 'All right, you're on,' she agreed, and wondered if she might deliberately try to seduce Nathan again herself, merely so that Celeste could win her bet.

Celeste put down her sherry, her eyes glistening. 'I...I think I might go and freshen up,' she said a little shakily. 'Would you mind going and asking your father what time he wants us ready for dinner, and remind him to make a booking to wherever he's taking us?'

Gemma found Byron relaxing on a lounger under a tree, Jaws stretched out by his side and thoroughly enjoying a gentle stroking of his ears.

'Don't get up,' she said as she approached and pulled up a deckchair to sit down beside him. 'Celeste said to remind you to book the restaurant. She also wants to know when you want us ready by.'

'No need to book on a Monday night,' he returned confidently before glancing at his watch. 'It's twenty after five now. How about we leave around seven?'

'Sounds good to me.'

'Can't understand why Nathan doesn't get along with this dog,' Byron puzzled aloud. 'He's as gentle as a lamb.'

'I think it might have something to do with his never having had a dog or a pet when he was a boy,' Gemma tried to explain. 'He never developed any rapport with animals and an animal can sense that. I'll bet you had a pet as a boy.'

Byron seemed to ponder this, nodding slowly up and down. 'Yes, you're right. I had a lot of pets over the years, including a dog once. He was a Labrador, a big fat lazy dog, and I loved him to death.'

'Nathan never had anything to love as a child except an unstable nymphomaniac who couldn't possibly have given him a good example of what real love was like. He's been struggling ever since to learn how to really love, especially when it comes to women. Nathan's idea of intimacy begins and ends with the physical.'

Byron sighed. 'I had hoped he might have thrown off that evil bitch's influence by now,' he muttered. 'It wasn't his body she corrupted, it was his view of himself as a male.'

Gemma frowned. 'Are you talking about Nathan's mother?'

'No, though, as you say, she's got plenty to answer for as well. I'm talking about Lorna Manson.'

'Oh, *her*.'

Byron's eyes snapped round in surprise. 'You *know* about Lorna?'

Gemma nodded. 'I'd heard rumours from Ava but it was Nathan who told me the grisly details. That woman as good as raped him!'

'Yes, she did, but it was the eventual rape of his mind that did the most harm. Did you know that bitch used to tell him he was a bad seed, just like his mother? That he'd inherited her weakness for sex and that no woman would ever want him for anything else but sex, just as no man have ever wanted his mother for anything other than sex.'

'Good God! No, I didn't know that.'

'I didn't think so. Nathan broke down and told me one night soon after I met him. He was quite drunk at the time. He kept telling me over and over that he wanted to be good, but he was afraid he was programmed to be bad.'

Gemma was appalled that anyone would play with a child's mind like that, especially one as vulnerable as Nathan would have been. But really, it explained so much. No wonder he'd gone off the rails after he did what he did to her. He would temporarily have thought he'd reverted to type, to the depraved and uncontrollable animal this Lorna person had tried to convince him he was.

Did he still think that? Gemma wondered. Was that why he too was trying hard to keep their relationship platonic for a while? Maybe he was trying to prove something to himself, not her. Still, knowing this made Gemma feel so much more confident that she was doing the right thing in not sleeping with Nathan. Her feminine intuition had steered her in the right direction, and, bet or no bet with Celeste, she vowed again to keep sex out of their relationship for a while longer.

'I did my best to convince him that wasn't true, of course,' Byron growled, 'and I genuinely thought I had gotten through to him. But maybe I didn't. Maybe down deep he still thinks he's not fit to be truly loved, that all he can offer a woman is what's between his legs. Oh, God, I'm sorry, Gemma. That was a crude thing to say. I forgot who I was talking to. Sorry.'

'You don't have to apologise. I appreciate your being frank with me. And I don't want you to worry about Nathan. He'll be fine. *We'll* be fine.'

Byron shook his head. 'You're such an optimist. Either that or you're as stubborn as a mule.'

Gemma grinned. 'Do I get that from my father or my mother?'

'Oh, definitely your mother. That woman would try the patience of a saint. She—'

'What is this?' Celeste loomed up over them suddenly, hands on hips, face full of exasperation. 'I send Gemma down here to find out a couple of simple things and she's gone a week! Hello, dog,' she added, idly patting Jaws who had stood up and had started nudging his nose against her hand.

'I think he likes her too,' Byron told Gemma drily.

'I think he does. Nathan's going to spit.'

'I'm the one who's going to spit if I don't get a straight answer.'

'To what, darling?' Byron asked with mock innocence.

'To what you two are up to, huddled together down here all this time. What's so engrossing?'

'We were discussing dogs, actually,' Byron said, 'well, bitches to be more precise.'

Celeste looked perplexed. 'But Jaws here is a dog dog. Isn't he?' She peered under him to make sure. 'Yes, he is.'

'I was thinking of getting him a companion so that he won't be lonely,' Gemma said in support of Byron's distortion of the truth.

'Better to take him to the vet,' was Celeste's advice. 'Have him fixed up.'

'Ouch!' Byron exclaimed. 'Did you hear that, Jaws? Better start running, lad.' Giving the dog one last pat, he stood up. 'I suppose I'd better go and have another shave before we go out.'

Celeste watched him go with suspicion on her face. 'Why do I get the feeling I've just been lied to?'

Gemma looked at her mother and made a decision. 'Perhaps because you have. No, don't get mad. Byron was just protecting Nathan.'

'Protecting Nathan? I . . . I don't understand.'

'No, I can appreciate that, and it's unfair to you to keep you in the dark. Nathan is your son-in-law and he's going to be your son-in-law for a long time so I think you deserve to know what has made him into the man he is today. But you have to promise me to listen with all the kindness and understanding that I know is in your heart. You pretend to be tough, Mother, but you're not. You're as much a softie as Jaws here . . .'

Some time later, Celeste lifted teary eyes to her daughter. 'I . . . I didn't realise . . . Oh, the poor boy . . .'

'He's not a boy any more, Mother. He's a man. A very decent and very good man. But he needs those around him to really believe in him for him to believe in himself. People say you have to love yourself to love others. I think Nathan finds it hard to love himself because of what that woman did to him at a crucial stage in his growing-up years.'

'That was wicked . . . what she used to tell him. Really wicked.'

'Yes, it was.'

'I . . . I want to call that bet off, Gemma. It . . . it's not nice. You do whatever you think right, darling. You seem so wise where Nathan is concerned. I'm sure you'll make the right decision. And you can have the Heart of Fire anyway. I want you to have it.'

Gemma slowly shook her head.

'But why not? I can afford it.'

'It's just a thing, Mother. I don't want things. Why don't you sell it? Give the money to Byron's charity for street kids. Let it do some good, not rot away in a safe somewhere.'

'Are you sure?'

'Yes, I'm dead sure. Oh, and Mother . . . I would still be honoured for you to name my baby.'

Celeste's eyes flooded with tears, her hands flying to cover her mouth in a vain attempt to stifle a sob. 'You don't know . . . how happy . . . you've made me,' she choked out.

Gemma went to total mush inside, her own eyes swimming. 'You don't know how happy you've made *me*,' she managed to get out before both women threw their arms around each other and wept.

CHAPTER THIRTEEN

BYRON and Celeste spoiled Gemma outrageously that week, not allowing her to cook a single meal and fussing over her like mad. The weather became steadily hotter and they spent most afternoons beside the pool before going out each evening to dinner.

In a way, by Friday, Gemma was relieved to see her parents go, sure that she must have put on a few kilos. With Ma's advice about alcohol in mind, she'd refused to join in with all the sherry before dinner, wine with every meal, then port as a nightcap before bed every night, but her soft-drink substitutes had been just as fattening. Celeste burnt her calories off, churning up and down the pool in endless laps, but Gemma had never been much of a swimmer, and it was too hot for long walks.

An inspection of her figure in the bathroom after her shower on the Thursday night had shown a definite all-over rounding in her curves. It also revealed what looked like a couple of stretch marks on the undersides of her breasts. The sight had upset her. God, what would she be like when her stomach started ballooning? Visions of wall-to-wall stretch marks, sagging breasts and saddlebags loomed in her mind, so as soon as Celeste and Byron drove off she dashed down to the shops and bought a video of exercises for pregnant ladies as well as a moisturising lotion guaranteed to keep her skin supple and elastic.

'You look tired,' was the first thing Nathan said when he walked in that evening shortly after seven. Jaws growled at him from in front of the television set, and Nathan scowled back. 'Just keep your distance, dog, and I'll keep mine.' He turned back to Gemma and gave her a peck on the cheek.

'So what have you been doing? I thought Byron and Celeste were supposed to be looking after you but you look exhausted.'

Gemma didn't want to tell him that she might have overdone things that afternoon with the exercise video, having only just stopped, so she simply shrugged. 'I...I haven't been sleeping well lately.'

His expression was rueful. 'That makes two of us. But seriously, Gemma, I hope you're looking after yourself properly.'

'Pregnant women aren't invalids, Nathan,' she snapped, annoyed with herself for looking at him and thinking sex immediately. But dear heaven, he did have that effect on her. Still, in her defence, he'd obviously had that effect on a lot of women. Mother Nature had given him the face and body of a golden god, in much the same way his mother had been a golden goddess. Even when he'd been only sixteen, he'd inspired uncontrollable lust in a woman old enough to know better.

But Lorna hadn't, and in the pursuit of that lust had almost destroyed Nathan's faith in himself as a human being. With this firmly in mind, Gemma renewed her vow to show Nathan how much she cared for *him*, the human being, not just the superstud.

Which she was hardly doing by snapping at him.

Remorse brought a silent groan before she managed to dredge up an apologetic smile.

'I probably look a bit hot and bothered because I've been in the kitchen, cooking. I know you said not to make dinner, since Kyle and Jade won't be here till late, but I couldn't stand the thought of going out to eat again, so I popped a chicken in the oven with some baked veggies. I hope you don't mind.'

'No,' he smiled warmly, and her heart flipped over. 'Why would I? I love your roast chicken dinners.'

'Good, then why don't you go put your feet up and I'll get you a drink? I can imagine what that drive up from Sydney is like, especially on a Friday night. What would you like? Coffee? Beer? Some white wine perhaps?' Having been a good little teetotaller all week, Gemma decided the odd glass of wine or two this weekend wouldn't hurt.

'What I'd like is for *you* to sit down while I get *you* a drink,' Nathan returned. 'Is there a bottle of wine in the fridge?'

'Lots and lots,' she admitted, thrilled by his consideration. 'I think Byron and Celeste are bordering on alcoholics.'

Nathan's laughter was dry. 'Could be. Something must be making them so happy together. I'd rather blame it on their being pickled all the time rather than disgustingly in love.'

Gemma's insides contracted at this last sarcastic remark. 'I don't think they're in love at all,' she said, and Nathan's head whipped round to stare at her.

'Why do you say that?'

'Because being ''in'' love sounds like a very temporary state, like an illness which they will soon develop an immunity for. They love each other, Nathan. They had loved each other for over twenty years.'

He snorted his scorn. 'I think good old lust has a strong hand in their feelings for each other. Byron can't keep his eyes off Celeste.'

'Or his hands.'

'Gemma!'

'But that doesn't mean they don't love each other, Nathan,' she argued hotly. 'Lust is just another side to love. I would hate to love a man and not lust after him as well.'

It was a brave thing to say, considering the man she was saying it to. Nathan's eyes narrowed, sweeping over her flushed face then down her suddenly breathless body which was, at that moment, encased in bright pink shorts and a matching T-shirt. Her hair was swept back up off her face in a rather haphazard pony-tail and her feet were bare. She wore no make up except a quick dash of pink lipstick.

'What about the reverse? Could you lust after a man yet not love him at all?' he asked with a sardonic arch of one brow.

'Yes,' she admitted. 'But not indefinitely. I would eventually want something more.'

'I wouldn't be too sure of that, Gemma,' he drawled. 'Lust, by its very nature, is a corruptive force. It can make one want all sorts of things. And *do* all sorts of things.'

Gemma's heart lurched. Was he just being cynical or was he delivering some sort of dark message?

'Why don't you sit down and put your feet up,' he went on brusquely, 'and I'll get you that glass of wine? I might have one myself. It's been one hell of a week.'

Gemma decided while he was uncorking the bottle and pouring them each a glass that she would not try to find some secret message in what he just said. It was probably just an instinctive remark, born from his troubled past. But it underlined his ongoing mistrust of his own emotions, and perhaps hers. What would it take, she wondered and worried, for him to believe she loved him, and that he loved her?

For they did love each other. If they didn't, they wouldn't be here at this very moment. Together.

Yet Gemma's own certainty about their feelings did not give her peace of mind. If anything, it brought an added burden not to foul things up, not to do anything to spoil what they could have together for the rest of their lives, as long as she didn't do anything stupid at this juncture. It came to her with a stab of dismay that Nathan didn't need to see her lusting after him in any way, shape or form. She had been crazy even to bring up the subject of lust.

'Thank you,' she said crisply when he handed her the glass and settled himself into the chair opposite. Jaws, who was lying on the rug not far from Nathan's feet, gave him a filthy look and crawled closer to Gemma.

'I see I'm still as popular as ever,' he bit out. 'I suppose he drooled all over Byron and Celeste.'

'Well, not exactly drooled . . .'

'But he didn't try to turn them into Long John Silvers.'

'Er—no . . .'

'I thought not. It's said animals have an instinct about people. Do you think he's trying to tell you something about me?'

'Only that you're as wary of him as he is of you. One day you'll look at each other and decide how foolish you've been not to be friends.'

Nathan chuckled. 'That'll be the day.'

The telephone rang. 'I'll answer it,' Gemma offered, putting down her wine and getting to her feet.

The telephone was at the end of the kitchen counter.

'Hello?' she answered.

'Gemma, it's Kyle. Problems this end, I'm afraid, so we won't be up. Jade had a bit of a dizzy turn at work today and the doc has ordered complete bed rest over the weekend.'

Gemma frowned her concern. 'She's really all right though, isn't she?' Jade was nearly eight months pregnant and in Gemma's opinion shouldn't be at work anyway. But there was no telling Jade what to do.

'Yes, she's fine. Naturally, I've been trying to get her to delegate at work till after the baby's born but what with Byron having been away she felt she had to go in every day. Still, Byron will be back on deck come Monday and I think between us we should be able to persuade her to take it easy from now on. So how are *you* keeping, love? Nathan tells us you haven't been tippy-top either.'

'Oh, I'm not too bad. I still get the odd spot of morning sickness but my doctor says that should hopefully pass off soon.'

'I must say I've never seen a man as emotional about his wife expecting as Nathan was when he told us,' Kyle commented. 'You know, Gemma, people sometimes get the wrong impression of Nathan. He seems very cool and controlled but might I say from personal experience that it's often the men who seem the most cool and controlled who underneath are the least?'

'I know what you're saying, Kyle, and I think you're probably quite right.'

'Jade wanted me to pass a message on to you specifically. She said to tell you to be gentle with Nathan, whatever that means. I would have thought she should be saying that to him. You're the one who's pregnant. Still, you know

Jade. She works on instinct and intuition so perhaps you should listen to what she says.'

'I will, Kyle. I will.'

'I'd better go, Gemma. I have to pop down the corner shop for some assorted chocolate bars. Madam Mother-to-be has a case of the fancies. Has that struck you yet?'

'Not yet.'

'It will,' he sighed. 'I'll have to give Nathan a list of items to have on hand so that he doesn't have to go roaming the streets in the middle of the night in search of an all-hours shop. Has he arrived there yet, by the way?'

'Yes, a few minutes ago.'

'Looks like it'll just be the two of you for the weekend, then.'

'Yes.'

'I doubt Nathan will mind that,' he chuckled. 'Well, bye now, sweetie. Look after yourself.'

'You too, Kyle. Bye.'

Gemma hung up and turned to find Nathan looking over at her with frustration on his face. 'Don't tell me,' he growled. 'They can't make it.'

'Jade had a dizzy spell at work and the doctor's confined her to bed for a couple of days.'

'Stupid damned girl! Why doesn't she ease up a little? I'll bet she'll be back at that miserable desk at Whitmore's within days of the baby being born. I can't understand women who have babies then don't want to stay home and look after them.'

'Don't be so narrow-minded, Nathan. Jade won't neglect her baby. Kyle would have something to say if she did. But she has a right to work if that's what she wants to do.'

'What are you saying, Gemma?' he returned sharply. 'That you will want to go back to work after our baby is born?'

'No, I'm not saying that at all! I've always planned on being a full-time mother. I also planned on having a lot more than one child.'

Nathan's eyes rounded a little. 'How many did you have in mind?'

Gemma shrugged. 'Oh, I don't know. Five or six.'

'Five or six!' Nathan shot forward on the chair, his wine almost spilling. 'Good God, woman, I'm thirty-six years old.'

'Yes, I know,' she returned quite calmly. 'But I'm only twenty. And it's me who has to have them, Nathan. Your part of the process won't take much out of you, will it? Besides, I thought you liked being a father.'

Nathan slumped back into the chair, looking stunned for a few seconds before his face slowly cleared of shock and he looked up at her, grey eyes steely. 'I think we'd better take this one baby at a time, don't you?' he said, and abruptly stood up. 'I'm going down to the study to work. Call me when dinner's ready.'

Gemma watched, taken aback, as Nathan strode down the hallway and disappeared into his private cave. The slamming of the door behind him obliterated the sense of optimism that had been growing in her heart since Nathan arrived. Now she saw that nothing had been solved yet. Not in Nathan's eyes. He was still as unsure of their relationship as he had always been. Maybe he still believed her feelings for him were bound up in lust. Maybe he thought she was still too young to be truly in love. Who knew what he damned well thought?

From that moment on, the weekend was ghastly. Nathan came out of the study only to eat and go to the bathroom. His behaviour propelled Gemma back to their honeymoon, when, out of the blue, he'd started writing, his complete absorption in his work bringing their honeymoon to an abrupt end. This time, there was no honeymoon to terminate, but Gemma still felt just as hurt, just as rejected. She'd thought they had gradually been reaching out to each other since she had come back from Lightning Ridge and now, suddenly, all their progress seemed to have come to nothing.

By Sunday afternoon, frustration and anger sent her storming out of the house and down the beach which was, unfortunately, far from deserted. Gemma felt like stomping along the sand, kicking it up and generally taking her feelings out on her physical surrounds. Instead, she had to carefully sidestep her way around sunbathing bodies till she was at the water's edge, where she tried to cool her temper and her toes at the same time. If she'd had her swimming costume on, she might have gone further, but she hadn't thought of changing her shorts and top for a bikini.

'Mrs Whitmore? Is that you?'

Gemma spun round at the highly unfamiliar male voice to stare into a vaguely familiar male face. She frowned as she struggled for recognition. He was thirtyish. Not an overly handsome man, but a well built one, with an interesting face, if a little hard.

'It's Luke Barton, Mrs Whitmore,' he told her, a charming smile softening his features in a very attractive manner. 'From Campbell Jewels.'

Of course! The man who had rescued her from Damian that awful night.

His intelligent grey eyes flicked down her bare legs and up again, not bothering to hide his admiration. But there was no leering in his gaze and Gemma smiled back. 'Yes, I know who you are,' she said warmly. 'And I know what you did for me. I never did thank you properly, Mr Barton.'

'Your husband did.'

'Aah, yes, my husband,' she said a little coldly.

Luke Barton seemed to pick up on her coolness, his expression turning speculative. 'Are you up here on holiday?' he asked.

'No. I'm not on holiday. I live here now. And no, Nathan and I haven't split up,' she added before he jumped to conclusions. 'He lives down in Sydney during the week and joins me here on the weekend. He's busy writing at the moment.'

'I see. I'm on holiday till the New Year, thank God. The boss has been away for a month and it's been bedlam without her, but she's back on deck tomorrow.'

'Yes, I know,' Gemma said, grinning at his surprise. 'Celeste's my mother-in-law, now that she's married to Byron.' There was no need to go into the more private tangles of their family relationships.

'Good lord, so she is!'

They laughed together, Gemma thinking he didn't know the half of it. They were standing there in the shallows, still laughing, when one of those rogue waves hit, totally soaking them both. It didn't matter with Luke, since he was only wearing swimming trunks, but Gemma's clothes were not the water-resistant type, their material going all soggy when wet, clinging to her in clumps.

'Oh, yuk!' she exclaimed, flicking the salty water off her fingers and flapping her T-shirt away from her chest. 'I'll have to go home and change.'

'Is it far? I'll walk with you. Maybe you could get your costume and we could go for a swim together.'

Gemma didn't have to think too hard to know what Nathan's reaction to that suggestion would be. 'Er—I think not, Luke. I can call you Luke, can't I?'

'If I call you Gemma,' he countered with that engaging smile of his.

'I don't see why not.' And suddenly, she didn't! Why should she be feeling guilty about talking to this man, or walking with him, or even swimming with him? He wasn't a stranger, and he had already proved himself a decent human being, a trustworthy human being. Despite what had happened with Damian, she had not become a total cynic. She still believed there were good people about—unlike Nathan, who didn't, especially in the male gender. But she couldn't spend the rest of her life avoiding male company just because Nathan might worry, or get angry, or jealous. That was no way to live. That was like being in a self-imposed prison.

'Of course you can call me Gemma,' she chided gently. 'I certainly don't want you calling me Mrs Whitmore all the time. Come on, this way. The house isn't far. It's just over on the side of that hill there. We'll go and surprise Nathan.'

Surprise was not exactly how Gemma would have described Nathan's reaction to her bringing home a semi-naked Luke Barton. Her husband's manners were perfectly polite, but she felt the underlying chill. Luke didn't seem to, however, and perched up on one of the kitchen stools, chatting away to Nathan about his play which he'd been to see the previous week.

'I took my sister, Mandy,' he said. 'She recently split with her boyfriend and was feeling down so I thought a night at the theatre would give her a lift.' He chuckled. 'A *lift*! It blew her mind away. Truly, she couldn't stop talking about it afterwards. Or should I say, she couldn't stop talking about the leading man? Personally, I thought the leading lady was much more eye-catching. But then I would, wouldn't I?' he grinned.

'Lenore's my ex-wife,' Nathan said drily.

'Really?' Luke's startled gaze slid from Nathan to Gemma, who was trying to relax, but couldn't.

'I must get back to my writing,' Nathan said on finishing the cup of coffee Gemma had originally cajoled him into having with them both. 'Nice to see you again, Luke.'

'I thought I might go back to the beach with Luke for a swim,' Gemma said quickly, and held her breath.

Nathan seemed to freeze for just a second before he turned to look over his shoulder at them both. 'In that case keep an eye on her, Luke,' he said. 'She's not the best of swimmers, are you, Gemma?'

'Er—no, I'm not.'

'I'll look after her,' Luke reassured.

'I sincerely hope so.'

Was Gemma imagining it, or had there been a dark warning in Nathan's parting words? Whatever, Luke seemed less comfortable with her after that, keeping his distance and not saying or doing anything that could even remotely be considered flirtatious. Gemma found that any enjoyment in his company had been spoiled, though maybe this was more tension on her part than on Luke's. In the end they parted company, Luke going off with some girl who'd been eyeing him up, and Gemma, relieved to go home alone.

Relief was also Luke's reaction, though he hid it well. He'd been a fool to go back to that house with Gemma Whitmore, especially knowing her husband was there. A man needed his brains tested! He'd seen for himself the sort of feelings Nathan Whitmore harboured for his wife the night he'd brought her home. He wasn't the sort of husband who would take to any male admiring his wife, even from a distance. He looked cool on the surface but there was an underlying emotional intensity about him that could be quite frightening.

Luke berated himself for being so stupid. It wasn't as though he'd been looking for any serious involvement with the woman. She was lovely to look at but really not his type at all. His type was smiling at him right now. Late twenties, a brunette, a go-getter who didn't want to be tied down any more than he did. Taking her hand in his, he drew her, laughing, into the waves, any thought of Gemma and Nathan Whitmore instantly behind him.

Nathan seemed to know the moment she walked in the door, for when she went into the kitchen to pour herself a glass of wine he materialised behind her.

'Have a nice swim?' he asked.

'All right, I guess,' she replied somewhat curtly.

'Luke up here on holidays, is he?'

'Yes, he is.'

'I don't want you going out with him.'

Gemma turned to look Nathan straight in the eye. 'I'm a married woman. I wouldn't go *out* with any man. But if I see Luke down the street or on the beach, I'll talk to him.'

'And swim with him? And bring him back here for coffee?'

'Maybe.'

'I don't want you to do that.'

'Do what?'

'Bring him back here for coffee. I don't want you being alone with him.'

'Why not, Nathan? Don't you trust me?'

'It's not a matter of trusting you. I don't trust the situation. Luke's a modern man and he fancies you.'

'But I don't fancy him.'

'You might . . . in the right circumstances.'

'My God, what kind of a woman do you think I am?'

'A very frustrated one, I would imagine.'

She glared at him, fury and, yes, frustration sending the blood pounding through her veins. 'Well, maybe I am but that doesn't mean I'd seek solace in the arms of another man. Sex isn't the most important thing in the world, Nathan. Neither is it necessary for one's sanity. I can do without if you can.'

'Maybe I can't any more,' he muttered, his face darkening. 'Maybe I can't stand another minute of being around you and not having you.'

'Then you know what to do, don't you?' she flung at him.

'Yes,' he snarled. 'I do!'

Gemma stood there, breathless with anticipation, her pulse-rate soaring at the way he started looking at her. An uncontrollable passion zoomed in his eyes, quickly followed by an oddly heart-rending torment. Then he did something that stunned her. He strode over to the refrigerator, snatched up his car keys from the top, and charged out of the house.

When she heard the car engine start up she raced out on to the front balcony but he was already reversing out of the driveway. She called out to him but if he heard her he ignored her shouts, burning rubber as he accelerated off up the street.

He'll come back, she told herself shakily. He's left his writing and his clothes behind. He's sure to come back once he's cooled down.

But he didn't come back. Dusk came and there was no sign of the Mercedes, or Nathan. Depressed, Gemma fed Jaws then brought him inside. The dog seemed to sense her mood, lying quietly at her feet when she settled down to watch the television blankly, unable to eat, unable to do anything except mentally castigate herself over everything she had done wrong.

She had been insensitive over the Luke issue. Of course Nathan would feel a little insecure at the moment. Why hadn't she reassured him instead of goading him? God, but she was an idiot!

Seven o'clock came and went. Eight o'clock. Nine.

He definitely wasn't going to come back. Gemma put Jaws outside for the night, having stopped letting him sleep in her room this past week after she'd found a couple of fleas in her bed one night. She locked up the back door then tried Nathan's Sydney number, but there was no answer. Maybe he was there but refused to answer, knowing it would be her. Maybe he was punishing her. If he was, it was working.

In tears by now, she forced herself to have a shower, letting her misery wash down with the water. Afterwards, she dried herself then reached for the moisturiser she had bought, pouring a big dollop on to each breast, then working it in with a slow circular motion, her mind a million miles away.

When her eyes gradually refocused, Nathan's reflection was suddenly there before her in the vanity mirror. Shock sent her spinning round, the bottle of lotion slipping from her fingers on to the bathmat at her feet. 'You ... you came back,' she gasped.

Nathan said nothing, simply stared at her naked body for some agonisingly long moments, especially at her oiled breasts with their darkly glistening nipples. Stepping forward, he bent to pick up the bottle, his face betraying nothing of his thoughts or his intentions as he straightened to stare at her some more. She couldn't seem to move, or breathe, a hot flush suffusing her body as his gaze swept over it once more.

'I think ...' he said slowly, and tipped the bottle sideways, letting the creamy fluid pool in the palm of his hand ' ... that you should let me finish what you started.'

CHAPTER FOURTEEN

'CAN'T have my wife reduced to making love to herself,' Nathan went on in a low but seemingly calm voice, putting the bottle down on the vanity.

'But I wasn't!' Gemma protested huskily, her head whirling. 'I...I...'

'Sssh. Let *me*.' He dipped the fingertips of his right hand into the pool of cream and began smoothing it over her breasts, making her breath catch in her throat every time he grazed over one of her nipples. When the cream was all gone and he started using both his hands, massaging her, his thumbs rubbing over both tender peaks at the same time, she moaned softly and closed her eyes.

Dear God, but she had wanted this for so long. Please don't let him stop...

He stopped, but only momentarily, pouring more of the lotion into his hand and spreading it over her stomach. Gemma experienced a temporary pang of disappointment that he had abandoned her breasts. They were so deliciously swollen and sensitive by now and craved even more attention. But soon, the focus of her desires shifted, especially when Nathan started smoothing his oil-slicked hands down over her thighs.

'Move your legs apart,' he ordered.

Gemma blinked, lifting a flushed face to his oh, so cool one. The sight of his controlled countenance was like having a bucket of cold water thrown over her. Was this an example of the control he'd once vowed to have over his sexual desires in future? Or was it that he thought he had to be calm and careful, because she was pregnant?

Gemma didn't want him calm and careful. She wanted him as passionate as he had always been. She wanted him to want her and need her and love her so much that there was no room for erotic techniques or one-sided foreplay. She wanted him to strip off his clothes and reach for her with shaking hands, wanted him to kiss her till they were both mindless with the yearning to come together as men and women had been coming together since Adam and Eve.

It was on the tip of her tongue to say as much, her face perhaps betraying her feelings, when he did step forward and take her in his arms, capturing her mouth with a kiss that distracted her from her growing dissatisfaction. His lips were demanding, the hands sliding down her back equally so as they curved around her buttocks, lifting her body to mould against his.

The feel of his stark arousal pressing against her stomach came as a shock. So he wasn't so controlled after all!

His desire refuelled her own, sending a low groan from deep within her throat. Her mouth flowered open, accepting the immediate thrust of his tongue. When he eased her legs slightly apart and started caressing her intimately, she was soon beyond wanting anything but the completion of the journey he was mercilessly setting her upon. When he stopped kissing her to scoop her up into his arms, his desertion was only brief, his mouth returning to keep the heat in her veins at fever pitch as he carried her quickly back into the bedroom and over to the waiting bed.

There, he laid her gently down, the kissing continuing while he ran tantalising hands down over her tingling flesh. She whimpered her distress when he left her to discard his own clothing, despite his not taking very long.

'Tell me you love me,' she urged blindly when he finally covered her naked flesh with his.

His hesitation was marked, and it drove her crazy. 'Just say it!' she cried, and raked her nails down his back.

He gasped and rolled over, carrying her with him so that she was lying on top. Her hair fell around her face and she swept it back with a shaking hand. 'Why won't you tell me you love me?' she challenged. 'You do, you know, the same way I love you.'

'Is that so?' he said scoffingly. 'How do you know? Don't count on what you're feeling at this moment. That's not love. I could make any number of women feel exactly the same way.'

Outraged, Gemma went to lever herself up off him, but he grabbed her wrists and held them wide so she collapsed on his chest again. She glared down into his face which was only inches from hers. 'You're a bastard, do you know that?'

'Yes.'

'I . . . I hate you!'

His smile was wry. 'Now you're really lying. You don't hate me, Gemma, though perhaps you have every reason to. You still want me. That's one of the reasons why you came back to Sydney with me. The baby might have been the main reason, but this is the other. Calling it love won't change the harsh reality of the sexual chemistry between us. Forcing me to say I love you is just as hypocritical. Now why don't you shut up, my darling? I came back to make love to you, not to argue with you.'

'Why?'

'Why what?'

'Why did you come back to make love to me? Was it because you were afraid if you didn't I'd have an affair with Luke Barton?'

'Partly.'

'And what's the other part?'

'You need to ask? God,' he laughed. 'I've been climbing the walls this weekend with wanting to make love to you. Lord knows how I survived it. Writing doesn't even work any more. *This* is all that's going to make me feel human again.'

So saying, he let her wrists go, reaching down to curve his hands behind her knees, pulling them apart and forward till she was straddling him, her hips raised provocatively so that the apex of her desire was hovering above his. His face twisted in a type of anguish as his flesh probed hers, steel

into velvet, and then he was pulling her downwards, filling
her with his hardness, impaling her and holding her captive
in a grip of iron.

'For pity's sake don't move,' he commanded when she
began to struggle.

'But you're hurting me,' she protested.

His face showed shock and bewilderment.

'Around my hips,' she told him breathlessly.

'Aah...' He relaxed his finger-biting hold, rubbing her
flesh up and down. 'Sorry,' he rasped. 'I do get carried away
when I'm with you.'

'I know,' she said.

'Don't sound so smug,' he muttered. 'And do shut up. I
can't concentrate. You never used to talk when we made
love,' he growled, moving his pelvis slowly up and down.

Gemma's mouth opened on a sucked-in gasp of pleasure. She had never been on top before and found the sensations incredible. Compelled, she echoed his movements
with movements of her own. Nathan's moan of raw re-
sponse sent a hot dizzying excitement flooding through her,
making her want to hear that sound again, making her want
to send him wild. Quite instinctively, her insides contracted, and with her flesh gripping his tightly the experience soared beyond description.

'Oh, God,' Nathan muttered, almost as though in pain.

When he reached for her shoulders and tried to pull her
down to his mouth, she resisted, not wanting to stop what
she was doing. His hands slid down to her breasts instead,
playing with them as they rocked to and fro with her in-
creasingly frantic movements. Gemma had never experienced anything so compellingly exciting. Everything inside
her mind seemed to become focused on that part of her
body housing his, in the build-up of pressure that was agony and ecstasy combined. She would not have stopped if
the room had disintegrated around her.

'Yes,' she groaned when she felt her body tighten even
further. 'Yes,' she gasped when everything started explod-
ing in her head. 'Yes!' she cried aloud as her flesh followed, convulsing and contracting in a series of violent

spasms, propelling the male flesh within her to an equally cataclysmic climax.

It wasn't till several minutes after she had collapsed upon Nathan's chest and her breathing had almost returned to normal that an odd sense of unease crept in. Was it Nathan's silence that worried her, or the mention of her own wanton wildness? For a while there she had been totally lost in her own pleasure, uncaring of anything but the achieving of her own satisfaction. Was that love, or simply lust? Was Nathan lying there, thinking that she had just proved what he'd been saying all along, that what she felt for him was mostly physical.

When his lungs expanded then fell in a weary-sounding sigh, Gemma feared the worst. She felt impelled to say something; anything to break the awful tension that she imagined was slowly invading the room.

And then.

'Are you going to stay, Nathan?' she asked somewhat gingerly.

'The night, you mean?'

'No. Not just the night. Though of course I do want you to stay the night,' she added hastily.

'I thought you might,' came his dry comment.

'If you're not going to be directing the play any more,' she went on, staunchly ignoring the pain and panic his caustic words had evoked, 'couldn't you move up here to Avoca? It's where you wanted to live when we were first married. You don't have to sell the apartment at Elizabeth Bay if you don't want to. We could keep it as a Sydney base.' Gemma said this, though she didn't want to ever go back there. She'd never really been happy in that place.

'No, I think I'll sell it.'

Gemma smothered her intense sigh of relief. 'Whatever you like.'

'I'd like a shower,' he said bluntly. 'And I expect you to join me.' Cupping her face, he lifted it so that she was forced to look into his eyes. What she saw there horrified her. An almost bitter cynicism gleamed in that steely grey gaze, accompanied by a decidedly wicked resolve. She'd crossed an invisible line with him just now when it came to their sex life together and he didn't intend to let her go back. There would be no more virginal blushing. No more shrinking away from his more imaginative demands. No more 'I'd rather not's.

He clasped her close while he swung his legs carefully over the side of the bed. As he stood up, one arm moved down to cradle her buttocks, one wrapped tightly around her waist, supporting the full weight of her body. Which was just as well, she decided dazedly, since they were still fused together.

He carried her that way into the bathroom where he had her turn on the shower taps and adjust the temperature before he stepped inside the cubicle.

Gemma gasped as the hot jets of water cascaded over them both, Nathan moving their stance so that it mainly poured down between them, over his chest and her breasts. At this point he kissed her, uncaring that the water now splashed over their heads and poured down their backs. It was an incredibly erotic experience, especially when she began to feel his flesh stirring within hers again. She responded by tightening and releasing her internal muscles and would have stayed that way forever but he chose to withdraw and ease her down on to the floor.

Gemma took a moment to find her feet, a jelliness having invaded her thighs. Once she stopped swaying Nathan picked up a cake of soap and a sponge, lathered up the latter, then handed them both to her. 'Wash me, wench,' he commanded thickly.

Her hand shook when she started, moving the sponge tentatively over his chest at first. But gradually any shyness dissolved and, emboldened by her own escalating desire, her hand moved downwards till she was confronted with his quite stunning maleness. At this point she dropped the soap, groaning at her clumsiness.

'Leave it,' he rasped, then moaned when she lightly pressed the wet sponge against him, making another raw moan break from his lips.

God, but it drove her crazy to hear him moan like that. Now she enclosed the moist sponge around him more firmly and began sliding it up and down. He swore under his breath and braced himself against the tiled wall, his flesh quivering beneath her touch. Still, it wasn't enough for her. She wanted him to shudder with uncontrollable pleasure, wanted him to not be able to stop as she was never able to stop once he started making love to her. She wanted him to be hers, utterly and totally. Even if it was only this way.

'No!' he protested when she threw the sponge away and sank down on her knees before him, the water cascading over her head and down her body.

She ignored him, bending forward to kiss the top of each thigh before cupping the weight between them with her hands then planting softly teasing kisses up and down his straining body.

'Don't,' he groaned.

But she was without mercy or conscience, her own excitement and arousal so intense that what had once seemed like the ultimate in abandonment now seemed like the most natural thing in the world. She exulted in tantalising him with her tongue, to the way he trembled when she parted her lips and took him oh, so gently between them. Only an inch or two at first, then further and further till he was consumed totally within the hot cavern of her tender yet tormenting mouth.

When he seemed to freeze for a moment, she was suddenly overtaken by an urgency to propel him quickly over the edge, to make him surrender, if not his heart, then his body. She would not allow him to draw back, to retreat, to reject.

Her lips increased their pressure. Her hands found all sorts of intimate little places.

Suddenly, the water was snapped off and Gemma was being hauled upwards, lifted out of the shower cubicle, wrapped in a huge towel then carried back into the bedroom.

'If I thought you'd done any of that with any other man,' Nathan growled as he tipped her on to the bed and snapped the towel out from under her, 'I'd strangle you with my bare hands!'

Gemma took a few moments to find her voice, the blood still whirling in her head, her heartbeat racing with an arousal that refused to be either squashed or side-tracked. 'You know I haven't, Nathan,' she insisted huskily. 'You spoiled me for any other man. Quite deliberately, I imagine. You made me what I am. You made me totally and irrevocably yours. Don't tell me you're afraid of your own creation. This is what you always wanted me to be, isn't it? Your very own sex slave, ready to do whatever you want. Why did you stop me? Let me please you,' she pleaded, levering herself up on to her knees and wrapping her arms around his naked waist. 'Let me make love to you...'

She began by kissing the droplets of water that clung to his ribs, licking his skin dry as she gradually moved her mouth back down to his still throbbing desire.

'I want to do this, Nathan,' her lips whispered as they moved over him. 'And you want me to,' she rasped. 'Let me...'

He let her.

CHAPTER FIFTEEN

'DOESN'T Ava look beautiful?' Gemma sighed.

'All brides look beautiful,' Nathan returned, then slanted her a frowning look. 'Do you regret not having been a traditional bride with a traditional ceremony in a church?'

'In a way. It would be nice to look back on. But it's too late now, don't you think?' She smiled, patting her gently rounded stomach underneath her apricot silk sheath. She was just over four months pregnant, and beginning to show. She was also remarkably happy, had been ever since Nathan had moved back into her life as her husband two months previously.

At first she had been worried that their relationship hadn't changed, that it was still just a sexual thing, that he didn't really love her. But Ma had been right when she said what they needed together was time. With each passing day, Gemma became more convinced of the depth of their feelings for each other. Nathan might not have told her in so many words that he loved her, but he showed her every single day. Not only in his lovemaking, but in everything he did. Gemma could not have asked for a better or more considerate husband. Even Jaws had warmed to him, choosing to lie at Nathan's feet most nights in front of the television, instead of hers.

Of course it would be nice if he *did* say he loved her one of these days. But Gemma wasn't going to be greedy. Neither was she going to keep hoping for miracles. Clearly, Nathan didn't feel comfortable with the word love. Maybe he never would.

Her attention shifted back to Ava, who was standing in front of the altar looking up into Vince's face with a look of such heart-felt adoration that a lump immediately formed in Gemma's throat. When Ava actually started making her vows, her voice shaking with emotion, hot tears pricked at Gemma's eyes.

'I'm going to cry,' she warned Nathan.

'Don't you dare.'

'I am, I tell you,' she sniffled. 'I can't help it. Give me your handkerchief.'

'Haven't you got a tissue?'

'No. I didn't bring one.'

Sighing, he gave her the silk kerchief out of his breast pocket. Gemma blew her nose, at which Jade turned round from the pew in front of her. 'You're not crying, are you, Gemma?' she said accusingly. 'You *are*. God, that does it! I'm going to cry too now. Here, Kyle, take the baby. I'm about to dissolve into mush.'

Kyle was only too happy to take his precious Dominic into his arms, looking down into his sleeping son's face with even more adoration that Ava was looking into Vince's. Only a month old, Dominic Henry Gainsford already had his parents twisted around his chubby little fingers, so much so that Jade had put off the idea of having another child for a while.

Gemma had no such plans to spread out her babies. She intended having one after the other till her family was complete. She wanted her children close and she wanted lots of them. Maybe they'd have to sell the house at Avoca eventually and get a bigger place, but she wasn't going to worry Nathan with that thought just yet. He'd seemed startled enough by her original announcement that she wanted half a dozen children. She'd let him get used to that idea first before she dropped any more bombshells.

Having composed herself with thinking of her future family, Gemma refocused on the wedding ceremony, just in time to hear Ava and Vince being pronounced man and wife. It had been a very traditional ceremony, and a very moving one, so much so that Gemma did feel a pang of disappointment that she had never been a white bride with all the trimmings.

Still... her arm slipped through Nathan's and she smiled up into his handsome face... she really must stop wanting to have it all. She was already one of the luckiest girls in the world. One year ago she had come to Sydney with nothing. Since then she had found two wonderful parents in Byron and Celeste, fallen in love with a wonderful man in Nathan, gained a wonderful sister in Jade, and was now having a wonderful baby.

'We can sit down,' Nathan said once Vince and Ava moved over to start signing the register and marriage certificate.

Everyone sat down and immediately the organ music started, haunting in its angelic tones. Gemma glanced around the mêlée of guests. She hadn't met Vince's relatives till today, but there were enough of them to fill the groom's side of the church. The bride's side was not nearly so packed, though there were a lot more people than might have come to a wedding of Ava's six months ago. Since meeting Vince she had really blossomed, both in her personal life and her career. Her art exhibition the previous month had been an enormous success with her being touted as one of Australia's most exciting up-and-coming artists. Byron was so proud of her, as was everyone else in the family.

Gemma wished Melanie had been able to be here today. She'd been more of a friend to the Whitmores than a housekeeper, but since Melanie had just given birth to a baby girl three days before that was hardly possible. She and Royce had sounded ecstatic on the telephone, saying they had named the baby Tanya. They had also faithfully promised to make the trip out from England after Gemma's baby was born so that everyone could have a big get-together with their respective children.

Gemma wondered what sex her own baby would be. She and Nathan had decided not to ask when she had had her sixteen-week ultrasound. They wanted a surprise. As for names... since Gemma had given Celeste the privilege of naming her grandchild, she tried not to think of names she liked herself. All she could hope was that her mother didn't come up with anything too weird. If she did, they would just have to find a suitable nickname to use. No child of hers was going to have to go to school with a weird name!

'Byron tells me Celeste gave the Heart of Fire to the Australian Museum,' Nathan commented quietly as they sat there. 'He said she offered it to you but you didn't want it.'

'Yes, that's right, I didn't.'

'I suppose you're going to tell me that two-million-dollar black opal was just another *thing*,' he said drily.

'Well, it is, isn't it?'

'Only *you* would think that.'

She frowned up at him. 'Are you angry with me for not taking it?'

'I'm angry with you for being so damned right. I only hope I haven't done the wrong thing.'

'About what?'

'About something I've bought you.'

Gemma cringed inside. He hadn't bought her a single thing since they'd got back together again, except at Christmas, and she'd been very happy he hadn't. Finally, she'd begun to feel like a real wife, instead of an expensive mistress.

'What have you bought me?' she asked, trying not to look worried as she smiled and waved over at Lenore and Kirsty.

'Maybe I should have mentioned it earlier,' he hedged. 'Maybe I should have consulted you.'

'Nathan,' she said through gritted teeth, 'if you don't tell me this very moment, you can spend the night in the study. *Writing*!'

He gave her a look of such horror that she almost started to giggle. In truth, his writing output over the past two months had been so negligible that it was just as well he had inherited a fortune from his grandparents. It was also just as well that Cliff Overton had bought the Hollywood rights, not just to *The Woman in Black*, but a few other plays as well.

'Belleview,' he said, almost bleakly. 'I bought you Belleview.'

Gemma's mouth dropped open as she stared at him, her heart stopping, her eyes blurring.

'I thought you might like to live there,' he went on, his own eyes worried. 'You seemed so sad when you heard Byron was selling it. I thought... oh, hell, I've made another *faux pas*, haven't I?'

She shook her head and dabbed the tears away with his kerchief. 'You couldn't have done anything to make me happier,' she choked out.

'You mean it? You're not just saying that?'

Gemma's answer was really to burst into tears. Fortunately, her weeping was looked upon with indulgence by all and sundry. Why not? Most of Vince's Italian relatives were crying by this time anyway.

Nathan put an arm around her shoulders, drawing her against him. 'At last,' he sighed, 'I did something right.'

Gemma lay in bed later that night, tired but happy. The drive back from Sydney to Avoca after the reception had seemed very long and she was glad to get her clothes off, shower and tumble between cool sheets. February had been as hot as January, and, while there was a sea breeze wafting into the room, the house was still warm from being closed up all day.

'You were quick into bed,' Nathan teased as he came into the room, pulling at his bow-tie. 'Dare I hope that's a hint?'

'Come near me tonight and I'll have your guts for garters,' she warned, yawning.

'How's that for gratitude? I buy you a three-million-dollar mansion and I don't even get a reward.'

'I'll reward you in the morning.'

'I might be dead by morning.'

She pulled a face at him. 'Don't you ever take no for an answer?'

'No.' He ripped off his shirt to reveal his magnificent chest, tanned to a golden bronze from all the swimming he'd been doing. Gemma had always thought his body was beautiful with its wide shoulders that tapered down to slender hips and long lean legs. She especially liked his lack of body hair, his skin like satin beneath her hands.

When his hands dropped to undo the waistband of his trousers. Gemma began seriously to reassess her weariness. By the time he'd stripped off his trousers, throwing them on to a nearby chair, she'd rolled over to watch him avidly, slyly pulling the sheet down a little so that one dark ripe nipple peeped out at him. Gemma had long given up wearing any clothes in bed, having found it a waste of time. They were never on by morning.

Nathan's steely gaze travelled down to the stiffened peak, one eyebrow lifting. But he said nothing, merely stared for a moment then turned and walked into the *en-suite* bathroom. The shower jets came on in full force and Gemma rolled over on to her other side with a resigned sigh. Damn the man. It would be just like him not to touch her now that he'd stirred her interest. He could be contrary that way sometimes. Or was it that he always found her much more accommodating after he'd teased her for a while, after he'd made her wait?

She listened for the water to go off. When it did, she tensed a little. Any moment he would—hopefully—join her in the bed. He would curve his cool nude body around her back and start playing with her breasts. In no time, he would have her panting for him so that when he eased her legs apart and slipped into her she would be totally lost in a sea of desire. He'd been doing it that way lately, telling her it was less likely to disturb the baby. She'd found the position incredibly exciting, loving the feel of his hands on her while they were fused together.

God, just thinking about it was making her so hot and wet! She moaned softly in her need, aching for him.

And then he was there, scooping her back against him and taking her without preamble, exulting in her instant need for him, groaning his own pleasure when she started undulating frantically against him. They both rocketed to climax within seconds, leaving their mouths gasping wide, their chests heaving. Nathan stayed inside her, however, stroking her softly till their breathing calmed and that glorious feeling of peace washed through her. Her sigh was deep and full of satisfaction.

'You have a funny way of saying no,' he whispered, kissing her on the shoulder.

'Mmm.'

'How's Junior?' he asked, and started caressing her belly.

'Growing.'

'My God! Did you feel that? The little blighter moved. That's the second time this week.'

Gemma yawned. 'Probably protesting at all the action.'

'He'd better get used to it,' Nathan said drily. 'I'm not giving up his mother till the doctor orders it.'

'How do you know it's a he?'

'I don't, but *he* sounds better than *it*. Next week I'll use she. I'm an equal-opportunities father.'

Her laughter was soft and warm.

'Are you really happy about my buying Belleview, Gemma?' he asked. 'Naturally, we'll live here till the baby's born, since your doctor's up here, but then I thought we'd move back to Sydney during the week, and keep this place for weekends.'

She twisted her face around to look up into his eyes. 'That sounds wonderful. I love that house. And I love you.'

He kissed her. But he didn't say he loved her back. For the first time in ages, it really hurt. Perhaps he sensed her pain, for the kiss suddenly turned more hungry, his hands finding her most sensitive places till renewed desire obliterated everything and she ceased to think.

But only till it was over. Long afterwards, she lay wide awake in his arms, listening to his heavy rhythmic breathing and wondering if he would *ever* say he loved her again. Her thoughts went to Ava, who would also be lying in her husband's arms tonight. Vince would have told her he loved her. Gemma did not doubt that. He would have told her so many times that Ava would be dizzy with the words.

When Gemma finally fell asleep, her lashes and cheeks were wet. So was her pillow.

The first pains started when she was at home, alone. It was a Sunday, and only mid-June, with the baby not due for another two weeks. Nathan had driven to Sydney for the day to help Byron and Celeste move out of Belleview, since they had at last bought a unit they both liked.

At first Gemma thought it was just another backache. She'd had a few of those. But when the dull nagging ache suddenly turned into a gut-wrenching contraction, she knew the baby was on the way.

Trying not to panic, she dialled Belleview, only realising when there was no answer that she didn't know Byron's new number. Or even his address! Nathan had it written in his little black book but that went with him everywhere. When she tried Nathan's car phone, and received no answer on that either, she began to panic. For a few moments, she didn't know what to do or who to call.

'Jade!' she cried aloud, and rang her sister's number. Luckily, Jade was in.

'It's Gemma, Jade,' she said quickly, doing her best not to sound frightened. 'I've gone into labour and Nathan's not here. He's helping Byron and Celeste move today and I haven't got their number and . . . and . . .' Another contraction started and Gemma couldn't help gasping with the pain. It felt like something was sticking a knife into her and twisting it. 'Oh, God, Jade, the pain's bad. I mean, *really* bad.'

'I know, honey, I know. I couldn't believe it myself. Why do you think I'm not signing up for seconds in a hurry? Now you listen to me. Call a taxi straight away and get yourself to hospital quick smart. Which hospital are you booked into?'

'Gosford District.'

'Right. I'll find Nathan and the rest of them and send them straight to the hospital. When you get there, demand they give you every painkiller that God and man invented. And then some more. Forget all that natural-childbirth crap. I think men invented that idea out of revenge for us making them fathers. Now have you got all that?'

'Yes, Jade,' she whimpered, almost in tears with the pain.

'Now hang up and ring for that taxi, pronto.'

'I will.'

'Good girl.'

The taxi driver took one look at her, paled visibly, then bundled her into the back seat and drove as if the hounds of hell were after him. Fortunately, it being a Sunday in winter, there wasn't much traffic around and fifteen minutes later he was zooming up the ramp into Casualty, fortunately without killing both her and the baby. By this time, she was in a bad way indeed, one contraction hardly seeming to end before the next began, each successive one more intense. She kept biting her bottom lip in a vain attempt not to moan, but occasionally a small sound would sneak through.

Hunched over, she managed to make it inside, where the admitting nurse immediately called for a wheel-chair. Ten minutes later Gemma was lying in a hospital bed, showered and robed. She kept thinking the birth must be imminent, so when her doctor finally arrived and examined her, then told her that the birth could be some hours away, she stared at him in stark horror.

'I'm...I'm not sure I can stand this for that long,' she cried.

He patted her hand while he instructed the nurse to prepare an injection of pethidine. 'We'll do what we can to make you more comfortable, Gemma. First babies can be slow in making an appearance. It would help matters considerably if you would try to relax.'

Relax! How could she relax when her insides were being torn apart?

'You've been going to breathing classes, haven't you?' he said.

'Y...yes.' Her face twisted with pain, everything inside her tensing.

'Then pant during your contractions, deep even breathing in between. This should help as well...'

She hardly felt the needle in her thigh, yet she hated injections. The torment she was enduring put insignificant discomforts like injections into perspective. They could stick needles in her all over if only this agony would go away.

She wanted to cry, but pride kept the tears at bay. Women did this kind of thing every day. What was the matter with her? Was she extra-weak? A coward, perhaps? Or was there something wrong? Maybe the baby's head was too large. She wanted to ask the doctor all sorts of questions but he was called away to perform what he calmly called a 'Caesar'.

Images of their having to cut her open to get her baby out filled Gemma's mind. Oh, God, where was Nathan? Where was Celeste? She wanted her husband. She wanted her mother. She...

A type of haze suddenly began to infiltrate her mind. The pain was receding a little. Maybe she would live after all. She sighed, letting all the tension flow from her body. Fifteen minutes later, she began to feel like pushing.

When Nathan received the call from Jade, he nearly died. Gemma, in labour. His darling, all alone and possibly afraid. God, he could have killed himself for leaving her. He should have known something like this could possibly happen. Where were his brains?

Luckily, he'd been driving back to Belleview at the time, Jade catching him on his car phone as he approached the Mona Vale Road turnoff. Leaving instructions for her to call Byron and Celeste at their new unit in Mosman, he raced through the intersection and up the Pacific Highway, going north. Within minutes he was on the expressway. Nathan glanced briefly at the speed-limit and decided a fine was worth it. His foot came down and the Mercedes leapt forward.

Half an hour later he was screeching to a halt outside the hospital and racing inside.

'Maternity section!' he demanded breathlessly of the first nurse he saw. Taken aback but with a typical female reaction to Nathan, she dropped everything and showed him the way, even finding out what ward and room Mrs Gemma Whitmore had been placed in.

Nathan didn't know what to expect when he burst into the room. Certainly not an empty bed.

'She must be in Delivery,' the ward sister informed him when he cornered her at her desk. 'You'll have to be scrubbed, masked and gowned before you're allowed in there.'

'Then scrub, mask and gown me, woman. That's my life you're talking about!'

'Don't you mean wife?'

'No, dammit, I don't. And if anything bad happens to my Gemma I'm going to tear this hospital apart!'

'Push harder right in the middle of the next contraction,' the doctor instructed. 'Go with the flow.'

Gemma glanced over her shoulder at the delivery-room door, which was shut. 'Is my husband here yet?' she breathlessly asked the nurse for the umpteenth time, then screwed up her face as another fierce contraction took hold. 'Please,' she gasped. 'Please go and see . . .'

The nurse glanced down at the doctor, who nodded. She bustled out and Gemma tried to concentrate on pushing. But she had an awful feeling she was somehow holding on to this baby till Nathan arrived.

'Push, Gemma,' the doctor commanded, sounding annoyed with her.

The contraction eased off, and right at that moment Nathan was ushered in, the nurse still doing up the ties on his mask. 'Here he is, Mrs Whitmore.'

Nathan hurried over and took her nearest hand in both of his, anxiety and apology in his eyes. She smiled weakly up at him and would have said something if a contraction hadn't seized her at that moment.

Nathan was appalled at the agony on her face. When a smothered cry burst from her lips, the sound turned his insides.

'Push hard, Gemma,' the doctor said firmly. 'Push.'

Her fingers dug into Nathan's palms, the nails biting deep. But he said nothing, glad to share the pain she was obviously enduring, anything to lighten her load.

'That's good,' the doctor praised. 'A few more good pushes like that and it'll all be over.'

Nathan stared down at her pale tired face, at the dark rings under her eyes, at this beautiful brave young woman whom he loved more than life itself. Lord, how could he not have known how much he loved her? How could he have stupidly kept fearing it was only lust that moved him every time he looked at her?

There was no lust in him for her today. Only admiration and tenderness and caring. Only love.

He bent down and pressed his lips through the mask against her forehead. 'You can do it, darling,' he urged. 'You can do it . . .'

He saw her gather all her reserves of strength, saw her make another supreme effort, then another.

The sound of a baby crying took him by surprise. He'd almost forgotten about the child, his worry all for Gemma.

'You have a son, Mr Whitmore,' the doctor announced proudly. 'Here, Nurse, let Gemma hold her boy. She deserves it. She's had a pretty rough time.'

Nathan watched as all the exhaustion left Gemma's face, her eyes sparkling with maternal joy as her arms reached for her son. 'Oh, Nathan,' she cried, drawing the infant to her breast. 'Isn't he beautiful? Isn't he the most beautiful thing you've ever seen?'

Nathan swallowed. Yes, he thought. He had never seen anything as beautiful as his wife and son together. His heart squeezed tight for a moment when he thought of how his son had been conceived, but he quickly realised that none of what had happened in the past mattered any more. Nothing mattered but what he said and did from this day forward.

A resolution formed in his mind that he would marry his Gemma again. She would come to him down the aisle of a church, on her father's arm and dressed in white. Everyone would be there to watch them take solemn vows—even that ghastly old Ma—and afterwards they would have a fantastic reception before going away on a proper honeymoon then coming back to live happily ever after at Belleview. But the most important resolution of all was that he would not let a day go by without telling Gemma how much he loved her.

'What do you think Celeste will call him?' she asked, interrupting his train of thought.

'Alexander,' he said straight away. 'Your mother called me on the car phone while I was driving up here so that I could tell you. Alexander, if it was a boy, and Augusta if it was a girl.'

Gemma blinked up at him, then laughed. 'Thank God it was a boy.'

Nathan had to smile. 'Amen to that.'

'In that case pass me little Alexander,' the nurse said, smiling herself. 'I think he needs a bath and some clothes.' She carried him away, cooing and clucking.

Gemma sighed. 'I can see Alex is going to be a ladykiller. Just like his father.'

'I think he takes after his mother.'

'Oh? In what way?'

'By being instantly, infinitely lovable.'

Gemma's breath caught in her throat. It was so close to his saying he loved her. So close.

Nathan reefed the mask over his head, then bent down to kiss her on the lips, so softly that it was like feathers brushing over her mouth. 'Have I told you lately that I love you?' he murmured.

Her heart stopped. 'Not...not lately,' she managed to say in a strangled voice.

'I love you,' he said simply.

Gemma closed her eyes, then let out a shuddering sigh. How many moments could be as wonderful as this? How often did one have it all? How many miracles actually happened?

'I love you,' he repeated, his voice trembling.

HARLEQUIN ❤ PRESENTS®

Don't be late for the wedding!

Be sure to make a date in your diary for the happy event—
The seventh in our tantalizing new selection of stories...

Wedlocked!

Bonded in matrimony, torn by desire...

To Have and To Hold by Sally Wentworth
Harlequin Presents #1787

"Gripping and enticing..."—*Romantic Times*

Marriage to Rhys might seem the answer to all Alix's
dreams...after all, she'd fallen in love with him at first sight.

But Rhys only proposed to Alix because she'd make him
the *perfect* wife.

Then Alix decided to take control of her own destiny, and Rhys
found that he couldn't live without her!

Available in January wherever Harlequin books are sold.

MILLION DOLLAR SWEEPSTAKES (III)

SWP-H1295

A family feud…
A dangerous deception…
A secret love…

by Sara Wood

An exciting new trilogy from a
well-loved author…featuring romance,
revenge and secrets from the past.

Join Tanya, Mariann and Suzanne—three very special
women—as they search for their destiny. But their
journeys to love have very different results, as each
encounters the irresistible man of her dreams….

Coming next month:

Book 1—*Tangled Destinies*
Harlequin Presents #1790

Tanya had always idolized Istvan…well, he *was* her brother,
wasn't he? But at a family wedding, Tanya discovered a
dangerous secret…Istvan wasn't related to her at all!

Harlequin Presents: you'll want to know what happens next!

Available in January wherever Harlequin books are sold.

BRIDE'S BAY RESORT

UNLOCK THE DOOR TO GREAT ROMANCE
AT BRIDE'S BAY RESORT

Join Harlequin's new across-the-lines series, set in an exclusive hotel on an island off the coast of South Carolina.

Seven of your favorite authors will bring you exciting stories about fascinating heroes and heroines discovering love at Bride's Bay Resort.

Look for these fabulous stories coming to a store near you beginning in January 1996.

Harlequin American Romance #613 in January
Matchmaking Baby by Cathy Gillen Thacker

Harlequin Presents #1794 in February
Indiscretions by Robyn Donald

Harlequin Intrigue #362 in March
Love and Lies by Dawn Stewardson

Harlequin Romance #3404 in April
Make Believe Engagement by Day Leclaire

Harlequin Temptation #588 in May
Stranger in the Night by Roseanne Williams

Harlequin Superromance #695 in June
Married to a Stranger by Connie Bennett

Harlequin Historicals #324 in July
Dulcie's Gift by Ruth Langan

Visit Bride's Bay Resort each month wherever
Harlequin books are sold.

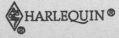

HARLEQUIN ®

BBAYG

Harlequin Romance ®
brings you

How the West Was Wooed!

Harlequin Romance would like to welcome you
Back to the Ranch again in 1996 with our new
miniseries, **Hitched!** We've rounded up twelve of our
most popular authors, and the result is a whole year
of romance, Western-style. Every month we'll be
bringing you a spirited, independent woman whose
heart is about to be lassoed by a rugged, handsome,
one-hundred-percent cowboy!

Watch for books branded **Hitched!** in the coming
months. We'll be featuring all your favorite
writers including, **Patricia Knoll, Ruth Jean Dale,
Rebecca Winters** and **Patricia Wilson**, to mention
a few!

HARLEQUIN PRESENTS®

Ever felt the excitement of a dangerous desire...?

The thrill of a feverish flirtation...?

Passion is guaranteed with the seventh in our new selection
of sensual stories.

Indulge in...

Dangerous Liaisons
Falling in love is a risky affair!

The Sister Swap by Susan Napier
Harlequin Presents #1788

Acclaimed author of *The Cruellest Lie*

It began as a daring deception....
But Anne hadn't bargained on living next door to
Hunter Lewis—a man who wanted to know *everything*
about her!

Still, Anne managed to keep up her act for a while. Until she
realized that hiding the truth from Hunter meant that she
was also hiding from love!

Available in January wherever Harlequin books are sold.

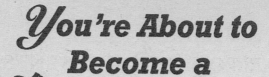

You're About to Become a

Privileged Woman

Reap the rewards of fabulous free gifts and benefits with proofs-of-purchase from Harlequin and Silhouette books

Pages & Privileges™

It's our way of thanking you for buying our books at your favorite retail stores.

PROOF OF PURCHASE
Offer expires October 31, 1996

**Harlequin and Silhouette—
the most privileged readers in the world!**

For more information about Harlequin and Silhouette's PAGES & PRIVILEGES program call the Pages & Privileges Benefits Desk: 1-503-794-2499

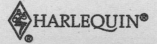